John Lydgate, Emil Otto J. Krausser

Lydgate's Complaint of the Black Knight

John Lydgate, Emil Otto J. Krausser

Lydgate's Complaint of the Black Knight

ISBN/EAN: 9783337299613

Printed in Europe, USA, Canada, Australia, Japan

Cover: Foto ©Andreas Hilbeck / pixelio.de

More available books at **www.hansebooks.com**

LYDGATE'S
COMPLAINT OF THE BLACK KNIGHT.

TEXT MIT EINLEITUNG UND ANMERKUNGEN.

INAUGURAL-DISSERTATION

ZUR

ERLANGUNG DER PHILOSOPHISCHEN DOCTORWÜRDE

DER

PHILOSOPHISCHEN FAKULTÄT DER UNIVERSITÄT
HEIDELBERG

EINGEREICHT

VON

EMIL KRAUSSER.

HALLE A. S.

DRUCK VON EHRHARDT KARRAS.

1896.

Sonderabdruck aus Anglia bd. 19, heft 2.

Einleitung.

Kapitel I.

Ueberlieferung des gedichtes.

Was zunächst den titel des vorliegenden gedichtes anbelangt, so behalte ich den titel: *Complaint of the Black Knight* bei, unter dem das gedicht am bekanntesten und in die litteraturgeschichte eingeführt ist. Ob Lydgate selbst seinem gedichte diesen titel beigelegt hat, darf bezweifelt werden, da in dem ganzen gedichte der klagende niemals als *knight* sondern stets als *man* angeführt wird. Ob er überhaupt seinem gedichte einen bestimmten titel gegeben hat, lässt sich bei der verschiedenheit der titel, die dem gedichte in den einzelnen handschriften und alten drucken beigelegt und die ich bei der beschreibung derselben anführen werde, mit sicherheit nicht entscheiden.

Die *Complaint of the Black Knight* ist uns in folgenden handschriften und alten *black-letter* drucken überliefert.

A. Handschriften.

1. F. = Fairfax 16 in der Bibliotheca Bodleiana zu Oxford. Pergamenthandschrift aus der mitte des 15. jahrh. (c. 1440—1450), eine menge Chaucer'scher und anderer dichter werke enthaltend. Ueber die orthographischen eigentümlichkeiten dieser wertvollen hs. hat Skeat in der einleitung zu seiner ausgabe von Chaucer's Minor Poems (p. XL) ausführlich gehandelt.

Die *Compl. of the Bl. Kn.* steht auf fol. 20b—30a. Der titel, in roter tinte geschrieben, lautet: *Complaynte of a louers*

1

lyfe, wozu durch eine spätere, kleinere hand (wahrscheinlich John Stowe's) *or of the blake knight* hinzugefügt wurde. Der index zu anfang der hs. hat den titel: *The complaynt of a lovers lyve,* daneben geschrieben *the blake knight.* Die majuskeln zu beginn der strophen sind in schwarzer tinte geschrieben und mit roten schnörkeln durchzogen. Die linien beginnen zumeist mit kleinen buchstaben. An dem rande zu vers 7 steht durch eine spätere hand das im texte fehlende *louwers* nachgetragen, ausserdem finden sich etliche kreuze neben den versen, um fehler anzudeuten.

Obwohl F auch nicht frei von fehlern und lücken ist, so ist es doch diejenige handschrift, welche den relativ besten text überliefert, weshalb sie auch als grundlage der gegenwärtigen ausgabe benutzt wurde. Näheres darüber siehe kap. III.

2. T = Tanner 346 in der Bibl. Bodl. zu Oxford. Pergamenthandschrift aus der ersten hälfte des 15. jahrh. Die einzelnen gedichte sind in zeitlich ziemlich auseinanderliegenden handschriften geschrieben. Während die älteste handschrift, in der Lydgate's *Temple of Glas* geschrieben, bis nahe an 1400 datiert (vgl. Dr. Macray's ansatz in Schick's einleitung zu seiner ausgabe des Temple of Glas E. E. T. S. e. s. 61 p. XVII), dürfte die *Compl. of the Bl. Kn.* wohl in einer der jüngsten handschriften und in dem zweiten viertel des 15. jahrh. geschrieben sein. Die *Compl.* steht auf fol. 48b—59a. Der titel, der durch eine spätere hand nachgetragen wurde, lautet: *The complaint of y* black Knight.* Am ende steht: *Explicit.* Die linien beginnen durchweg mit grossen buchstaben. Von orthographischen eigentümlichkeiten sind insbesondere des schreibers vorliebe für *i* & *y* an stelle von *e* in den endungen anzumerken z. b. hertis 8, bryddys 23, leuys 33, bokys 347: siluyr 26, watyr 37 u. ö. shyuyr 46, bittyr 109; euyn 194; awhapid 168, louyd 316; wepith 66, semyth 169, berith 308. Einige male findet sich auch *t* für *th* geschrieben, z. b. hat (= hath) 268, 300, 482, and cherysshet 301, eine eigentümlichkeit, die auch das bekannte Cambridger Ms. Gg 4. 27 aufweist (vgl. Furnivall: Temporary Preface to the six-text edition of Chaucer's Canterbury Tales Part I p. 56) und die den schreiber als dem Westmittelland oder Norden zugehörig erscheinen lassen.

3. D = Digby 181 in der Bibl. Bodl. zu Oxford. Papierhandschrift aus der mitte des 15. jahrh. c. 1450—1460. Unser
gedicht, in einer zierlichen kleinen hand geschrieben, steht
auf f. 31a—39a. Der titel lautet: *The man in þe erber.* Am
ende steht: *Explicit (Edorb qd).* Die bedeutung des in klammern hinzugefügten konnte noch nicht ganz festgestellt werden.
Macray im kataloge der Digby Mss. ist der ansicht, dass es
quod Brode zu lesen und *Brode* wahrscheinlich des „transcriber's
name" ist. Die linien beginnen mit grossen buchstaben. Der
schreiber zeigt eine grosse vorliebe für *i* & *y* statt *e* in den
endungen, ausserdem schreibt er *wordle* statt *worlde* 323, und
wordly statt *worldly* 493, eine metathese, die sich besonders
bei den südengl. schriftstellern bei Will. de Shoreham und Dan
Michel vorfindet (vgl. Wülker's Ae. Lesebuch I. S. 130. v. 52
und Kluge in Paul's Grdr. I. S. 859).

4. Arc. S. = Archiv Selden B. 24 in der Bibl. Bodl. zu
Oxford. Papierhandschrift aus den 70er jahren des 15. jahrh.
Auf seite 120 findet sich als datum 1472 angegeben. Ein
titel fehlt hier; am ende steht: *Here endith the maying and
disport of Chaucere.* Ausgelassen sind strophe 17 und 18. Wie
aus den orthographischen eigentümlichkeiten hervorgeht, ist
diese handschrift in Schottland geschrieben. Dieselbe ist auch
bekannt, dass sie als einzige hs. das berühmte *Kingis Quair*
des königs Jakob I. von Schottland bewahrt hat.

5. B = Bodley 638 in der Bibl. Bodl. zu Oxford. Papierhandschrift mit einer lage von pergament zu beginn und ende
der einzelnen lagen, geschrieben um die mitte der zweiten
hälfte des 15. jahrh. Die *Compl. of the Bl. Kn.* ist nicht vollständig überliefert. Der grösste teil des gedichtes ist ohne
zweifel beim binden der hs. verloren gegangen; nur das letzte
drittel von vers 468: *So doth this god with his sharp flon* an
ist erhalten und steht auf fol. 1—4. Der laufende titel in
roter tinte geschrieben, lautet: *The complaynte of a Louers
lyfe.* Am ende steht: *Eplicit the compleynt of a loveres life.*
Die linien beginnen mit grossen buchstaben.

6. S = Additional Ms 16165 des Britischen Museums.
Geschrieben um 1450 auf papier durch John Shirley († 1456),
wohlbekannt „as a transcriber and preserver of the works of
Chaucer and Lydgate". (Brooke Literatur Primer. p. 54.) Die
Compl. steht auf seite 190b—200b. Der titel lautet: *A com-*

playnte of an amorous knight. Am ende steht *Explicit.* Die linien beginnen durchweg mit grossen buchstaben. Ausgelassen sind strophe 60 und 88—93.

Diese handschrift ist für unser gedicht besonders dadurch von wichtigkeit, weil hier ausser in einem zu anfang der hs. stehenden und von Shirley gedichteten prologe Lydgate an vier stellen als verfasser genannt wird; 1. in der seitenüberschrift p. 191b — 192a: *þe complaynt of a knight made by Liddgate*; 2. zu p. 192b — 193a: *þe compleynt in love made by Liddgate*; 3. in der mitte von fol. 197a: *le voyre dyt Daun Johan* und 4. auf fol. 199b: *L'envoye of Daun John.*

Die Shirley'sche manier den text zu verderben, indem er an stelle der worte des dichters seine eigenen worte einsetzt, tritt auch im vorliegenden gedichte sehr störend auf. Die orthographischen eigentümlichkeiten Shirley's, seine *eo*'s für *e*, *eþe* für *eth*, *ff* für *f* etc. sind durch Furnivall's publicationen für die Chauer-Society bekannt, vgl. dazu noch Schick a. a. o. p. XXIII f.

7. P = Pepys 2006 in der Pepys-Library des Magdalene College zu Cambridge. Papierhandschrift aus der mitte des 15. jahrh. c. 1450—1460. Die *Compl.* steht auf fol. 1—17. Der titel, durch eine spätere hand hinzugefügt, lautet: *The complaynt of y* *blak knyght.* Am ende steht: *Explicit.* Der index zu anfang der hs., der durch eine saubere hand erst sehr spät nachgetragen wurde, hat den titel: *Complaint of the black knyght.* Folgende verse fehlen in der hs.: 221, 290, 415, 416. Die linien beginnen mit grossen buchstaben.

Das gedicht wurde sehr nachlässig geschrieben, auslassungen von wörtern und silben, umstellungen kommen sehr häufig vor und lassen diese hs. als eine der schlechtesten abschriften der *Compl.* erscheinen.

Die schreibereigentümlichkeiten, welche Schick a. a. o. p. XXI für den ersten teil des *Temple of Glas* angeführt hat, finden sich in der *Compl.* durch das ganze gedicht, und kennzeichnen den schreiber als einen Nordländer.

8. Asloane Ms. jetzt im besitze des Lord Talbot de Malahide in Dublin. Aus der vorrede zu dem von David Laing im jahre 1827 veranstalteten neudrucke des Chepman and Millar'schen druckes (vgl. unter B. 2) erfahren wir, dass: a

copy of it forms part of Asloans manuscript volume, which, along with other circumstances, renders it not improbable, that he may have employed his leisure hours in transcribing many of the pieces then in circulation, which had issued from the press of Chepman and Millar.

Dieses Asloane Ms. einzusehen, hatte ich keine gelegenheit. Eine ausführliche inhaltsangabe desselben giebt Schipper in seiner ausgabe Dunbars: *The Poems of William Dunbar, edited with Introduction.* Denkschriften der kaiserl. Akademie der Wissenschaften zu Wien. Phil.-histor. Kl. 1892. — Nr. 24. The mayng and disport of Chaucer (i. e. The Complaint of the black Knight) printed first by Chepman and Myllar 1508. (Only 61 seven line stanzas and the 2 eight line stanzas; the 17. and 18. stanza omitted; stanzas 51—81 lost) fol. 293—300.

B. Drucke.

1. W = Wynkyn de Worde's Druck. 4⁰.

Der druck ist ohne jahreszahl; angaben oder mutmassungen darüber konnte ich in keinem der *reference-books* wie Ames, Herbert, Dibdin finden.

Der druck hat ein besonderes titelblatt; es ist ein holzschnitt, einen baum darstellend, rechts davon ein junger und links ein alter mann. Darüber ist eine rolle mit dem titel: *The complainte of a louers lyfe.* Am ende steht: *Imprinted at London in the Flete Strete at the sygne of the Sonne by Wynkyn de Worde.*

Der Roxburghe Club veranstaltete im jahre 1818 einen wiederabdruck, den ich zur collation benutzt habe.

2. Ch = Chepman und Myllar's druck aus dem jahre 1508.

The knightly Tale of Golagros and Gawane and other Ancient Poems. Printed at Edinburgh by M. Chepman and M. Myllar in the year MDVIII. Es ist ein sammelband in klein 4⁰ von elf gedichten von Dunbar, Henrison und anderen, unter denen sich die *Compl.* als nr. VIII unter dem titel: *the Maying and Disport of Chaucer* findet. Dieser alte druck wurde im jahre 1788 durch *a medical gentleman, somewhere in Ayrshire* aufgefunden und der Advocates Library zu Edinburgh geschenkt. Eine facsimile-ausgabe des alten druckes veranstaltete David Laing, Edinburgh 1827.

An die *Compl.* angehängt, folgt ein Mariengedicht von 7 siebenzeiligen strophen. Die erste strophe lautet:

> Qwhen by dyvyne deliberatioun
> Of persons thre in a god hede yfere
> The grete message and hye legacioun
> Was send vnto that blyssit lady dere
> Be gabriel scho being in hir prayere
> Asking of god as prophetis dois exprime
> To send the son that shuld the warld redeme.

Am ende steht: *Explicit: heir endis the maying and disport of Chaucer. Imprentit in the south gait of Edinburgh be Walter chepman and Androw myllar the fourth day of aprile the yhere of god MCCCCC and VIII yheris.*

Von dem Mariengedicht sind nach Laing (preface p. 14) *two copies contained in Bannatyne's Manuscript, both of which are anonymous.* Man möchte einen augenblick versucht sein zu vermuten, dass dieses Mariengedicht etwa zu Lydgate's *Life of our Lady* gehöre. Doch ist dies nicht der fall; auch sind mehrere reime ganz unlydgatisch.

3. Th. = Thynne's Chaucer Ausgabe 1532.

Da im 16. jahrh. die *Compl.* Chaucer zugeschrieben wurde, so fand sie auch aufnahme in die erste gesamtausgabe Chaucer's durch Thynne und figuriert seitdem in allen alten Chaucerausgaben. Thynne's ausgabe hat folgenden titel: *The workes of Geffray Chaucer newly printed / with dyuers workes whiche were neuer in print before: As in the table more playnly dothe appere. Cum priuilegio printed by Thomas Godfray. London 1532.*

Die *Compl.* findet sich daselbst als nr. 17 gedruckt unter dem titel: *The complaynt of the blacke knyght.* Am ende steht *Explicit.*

Die späteren Chaucer-drucke gehen auf Thynne's druck zurück.

Kapitel II.
Das handschriftenverhältnis.

§ 1. Zwei gruppen von handschriften.

Die vorhandenen handschriften und ältesten drucke lassen sich in zwei gruppen teilen, eine gruppe X, vertreten durch

F, B, W, und eine Y, vertreten durch T, P, D, Th, S, Arc. S, Ch.,
wie aus den folgenden gegenüberstellungen deutlich hervorgeht.

20) my] f. X; 22) wolde] wol F, wyll W; 26) lik] lykyng F, lyenge
lyke W; 64) ther X] the Y; 70) icalled X] called Y; 87) Nat Y] That X;
94) pure] f. X; 121, 146) And Y] J X; 135) al this Y] as thus X; ful] f. X;
140) here Y] se X; 179) eke helpe X] helpe eke Y (h. now P. Arc. S.);
225) in Y] on X; 233) now colde] f. X; 241) his] f. X; 295) sight X] ryght
Y (light S); 299) more X; eny Y; 335) his^2] f. X (+ Th); 371) thes] f. X;
374) Tereus F (Terens W)] Theseus Y; 390) had Y] and X; 400) louers
X] lones Y; 405) most Y] must X: 421) false X] f. Y (— S); 453) of loue
X] aboue Y (— Th); 519) and X] if Y; 622) when Y] whom X; 666) to]
f. X; 671) him] f. X.

Diese charakteristischen lesarten in jeder der gruppen
werden zu gleicher zeit auch beweis genug sein, um zu zeigen,
dass keine derselben unmittelbar aus der anderen geflossen
ist. Wir haben daher anzunehmen, dass beide gruppen auf
eine gemeinsame grundlage zurückgehen, welche der geringen
abweichungen wegen, welche die beiden gruppen aufweisen,
vielleicht das original des gedichtes war.

§ 2.   Gruppe X = FBW.

Die nahe verwandtschaft der hss. F und B tritt wie bei
so vielen Chaucer'schen und anderer dichter werke, so auch
bei dem vorliegenden gedichte klar hervor. Ihnen schliesst
sich der druck Wynkyn de Worde's eng an, wie einerseits
aus dem gleichen titel: *Complainte of a louers lyfe,* der überschrift zu strophe 83: *Nota perseueranciam amantis* und zu
strophe 97: *l'envoye du quaer* erweislich ist, andererseits auch
aus der liste der übereinstimmungen in § 1, wozu noch weitere
hinzugefügt werden können:

BW: 480) wher] f.; 494) wyse] f. (+ S); 555) holy] holely (+ P);
560) so-euer] someuer; 678) and] but. — *F.B.* 603) leyth FB] ley W
(+ Y).

Trotz dieses engen zusammengehens ist jedoch keines aus
den andern geflossen. F kann nicht aus B und W stammen,
da F älter ist als die beiden andern; B und W sind nicht
aus F kopiert, da B und W an mehreren stellen im gegensatz
zu F die richtige lesart bieten (vgl. unten I.) und aus dem-
selben grunde kann auch W nicht aus B stammen (vgl. unten II.),
vielmehr gehen beide wie aus den oben angegebenen gemeinsamen lesarten ersichtlich ist, auf eine gemeinschaftliche vorlage zurück.

I. *B und W nicht aus F*: 15) I] f. F; 3'i) the] f. F; 32) her] the
F; 71) the] f.; 106) had] f.; 130) wher] ther; 176) helpe] now helpe;
187) of] to; 342) obey] wey; 348) pilers] periles; 358) al] as; 391) and] f.;
395) he] f.; 475) in] f.; 541) as] at; 628) O] of; 640) cause] f.; 670) be] f.;
681) myn] hym.

II. *W nicht aus B*: 581) languysshing] sanguisshing B; 640) take]
call B.

Da nun keiner der texte aus dem andern abgeleitet ist,
so müssen wir annehmen, dass sie auf eine gemeinsame grundlage (F B W) zurückgehen.

§ 3. Gruppe Y = (T, P, D, Th), (S, Arc. S, Ch).

Gemeinschaftliche lesarten, welche auf eine zusammengehörende gruppe dieser hs. und drucke hinweisen, sind ausser
den in § 1 angeführten noch folgende:

T, P, D, Th, Arc. S, Ch: 16) out stert] vp stert; 421) false] f. —
T, P, Th, S, Arc. S, Ch: 23) Into, die übrigen hs. Vnto. — *T, D, Th, S,
Arc. S, Ch*: 155) shall] shulde. — *D, Th, S, Arc. S, Ch*: 20) attelest] at
þe leste; 54) may longe] die übrigen hs. may not longe; 101) perse] die
übrigen hs. persyssh. — *P, D, S, Arc. S, Ch*: 139) al] f. — *D, Th, S, Arc. S*:
97) his] here. — *D, Th, Arc. S, Ch*: 281) non ne may] may noon.

Hierzu können noch etliche 30 weitere beispiele hinzugefügt werden, bei denen je drei oder zwei hs. übereinstimmen.
Wie ich schon in der überschrift zu diesem paragraphen
äusserlich kenntlich gemacht habe, lässt sich die ganze gruppe
in zwei untergruppen teilen, T, P, D, Th einerseits und S, Arc. S,
Ch andererseits. Diese abteilungen stammen keineswegs von
einander ab, was zu beweisen ein blick in die unter α und β
nun aufzuzählenden lesarten überflüssig machen wird; wir
haben also eine gemeinsame basis T, P, D, Th, S, Arc. S, Ch
anzunehmen.

α) Gruppe T, P, D, Th.

Die zusammengehörigkeit dieser hs. wird bewiesen durch
folgende übereinstimmungen:

81) gan spryng] came spryngyng; 216) loke] lokes; 414) nother]
nor; 617) doon] adoun; 647) werry wery] very.

Je drei hs. stimmen überein:

T, P, D: 6) the] f.; 108) welle] f.; 125) which] the which; 161) men]
man T, D, a man P; 173) therwith-al] therwith; 308) of Falshed] f.;
460) hit] f.; 505) also and] and also; 510) her] the. — T, P, Th: 252)
now] newe; 501) largesse] largenes. — P, T, Th: 674) go²] f.

Dazu kommen noch fälle, in denen je zwei hs. übereinstimmen.

T, P: 127) yude] Iende T, P; 136) he] f.; 168) amate] as amate
T, as mate P; 190) but²] so; 348) his] f.; 419) deth] of deth; 647)
hit] hit was. — T, D: 48) wreste] wraste; 414) ne] ne in; 567) wher]
whedyr. — T, Th: 52) celured] couered; 103) euermore] ouermore; 471)
so] to so. — P, D: 236) al] f.; 308) the] all the; 423) mony] many a;
599) pleynt] peyne. — P, Th: 351) ben] f.; 430) haunce] haunt. — D, Th:
577) a worde no] no worde; 669) trewe] f.

Trotz dieser ähnlichkeit ist jedoch kein ms. resp. druck
aus dem andern geflossen. T stammt nicht aus P noch D
noch Th, da T älter ist als die genannten; umgekehrt können
auch P, D, Th nicht von T abgeleitet sein, da sie an vielen
stellen gegen T die richtige lesart haben:

2) grene rede] red grene T; 14) the] to; 20) attelest] at leste;
33) to] f.; 42) this] the; 45) songe] they songe; 47) hyt] his; 60) lyte]
white; 73) yonge] fressh; 76) That] And; 122) a] in a; 138) malady]
lady; 147) priuely] peynyly; 148) in] f.; 150) so pitously gan] gan so
pitously to; 166] on the grounde in place desolate] and on the grounde
desolate; 168) Sole] So; 193] that] as; 210) be here now] he now here;
215) now] now and; 229) so meynt] ymeynt; 236) am] f.; 241) peyne]
hate; 253) arowes] arow; 273) lyve] lyen; 307) wrongfully] wrongwisly;
341) not refreyn] neuyr attayne; 360) Venus] Phebus; 362) his] this;
397) quyte hym so] so quit him; 402) men] man; 494) purveaunce] f.;
522) wille] f.; 527) mercie] f.; 562 u. 566) me] f.; 581) his] her; 593) fall]
yfalle; 595) swyftly] swythely; 600) dyd] can; 622) yow nur in T; 633)
wo] sorow; 656) he] ʒe; 666) to your] to you of youre.

P und Th sind auch nicht von D abgeleitet, da P und Th
in mehreren fällen gegen D die richtige lesart vertreten:

1) fresshe] f. D; 35) hem] hym; 42) grene] grete; 49) as] as she;
64) closed vnder] clothir; 66) wepeth euer of] euer wepith by; 73) oke
with] eke; 74) can] f.; 77) golde] colde; 124) her] f.; 125) of] f.; 127)
floures] erbis; 131) white] with; 143) no] ne; 158) speke] take;
169) that] f.; 178) O Niobe] Caliope; 191) haue no knowyng] no
knowyng haue; 191) suche] the; 194) like] f.; 195) that] f.; 212) deleful]
woful; 213) ful high] wofull; 218) sighes] thoughtis; 225) gronnde]
grownded; 227) is] f.; 234) colde as ise] as yse colde; 234) coles rede]
firy glede; 238) colde] hert; 256) Han] And hath; 264) Haue] hath;
279) do] to; 285) clepe] speke; 287) mordred] to mordir; 302) meneth]
movith; 331) the] þat; 339) was he] he was; 348) high] f.; 352) Be-set]
Sette; 353) sete] put; 366) trwe] Troy; 366) high] grete; 386) Adon]
Abdoun; 394) fre] and fre; 403) false] þe fals; 405) lust] love; 416) Ne]
No; 418) Nor] Not; 419) jupardy D] d. übrig. hs. in partyng; 441) that f.;
443) faute] defaute; 445) of] my; 459) no] ne; 471) so] and so; 493)
cure] f.; 509) make] f.; 523) yf that] f.; 523) saue] to saue; 539) your]

here; 570) deth my] f.; 579) myn] his; 604) for²] f.; 638) alle] the; 642) vp] f.; 644) Adoun] Abdomoun; 671) prouoked] promited; 675) my] f.; 676) shal] hath; 677) Such] Sche.

D und Th sind nicht von P abgeleitet, da sich bei ihnen die in P fehlenden verse finden.

Da nun keiner der überlieferten texte auf den andern zurückgeht, so ist anzunehmen, dass sie aus einer gemeinsamen quelle (T, P, D, Th) entsprossen sind.

β) Gruppe S, Arc. S, Ch.

Diese hs. nebst druck zeigen eine menge charakteristika, die darauf hinweisen, dass sie aus einer gemeinschaftlichen vorlage abgeleitet sind.

44) both] and; 49) brest] to brest; 58) Zepherus] Phebus Arc. S, Ch, feyre Phebus S; 62) that nur in S, Arc. S, Ch, 69) dovn] adowne (+ Th); 89) hide] abyde; 91) eueᵣe] euer hit; 128) gan] can; 173) yow do] do you (+ D); 180) that] þowe; 192) discryue] discerne; 196) beside] besyde him; 216) with ful] nur in dieser gruppe (ful f. Ch); 226) of²] f.; 230) shyuer] shele S, chill Arc. S, Ch; 245) will] wolde (+ T); 257) And] Of (+ W); 233) hete] hote (+ P); 290) So] f.; 292) ar] ben; 296) professed whilom] professit sum time Arc. S, Ch, some time professed S; 319) he hath] I haue; 337) ay] euer; 401) that love] he; 430) haunce] change (+ W); 485) euer saugh] sawe euer; 521) Yet] And; 547) vnto] nur in dieser gruppe; 549) welapayed (+ W), die übrigen hs. welpayed; 551) Vnto] To; 562) me I] I me; 663) to] for to.

Je zwei hs. stimmen überein:

S und Arc. S: 60) buddes] briddes; 86) ther nur in S, Arc. S; 142) what] what þat; 176) to] for to; 382) hir² nur in S, Arc. S; 394) his] her (+ P); 514) al] al maner; 523) ye] you (+ Th); 536) her] yow; 561) to] vnto; 577) a worde no] not oon word S, noght a word Arc. S.
— S und Ch: 405) lust] lustes.

Trotz dieser übereinstimmungen können die texte dieser gruppe nicht von einander abhängen, S nicht von Arc. S. und Ch, welche, wie ich unten zeigen werde, eng zusammengehören, da S die in Arc. S, Ch fehlenden verse überliefert, und umgekehrt können auch Arc. S, Ch nicht aus S abgeleitet sein, da sich die in S fehlenden verse in Arc. S, Ch finden. Ausserdem weist eine jede der hs. nebst druck eine menge von eigenen lesarten und fehlern auf, die von den anderen nicht geteilt werden. Wir müssen also eine gemeinsame vorlage (S, Arc. S, Ch) annehmen.

Als das hervorstechendste merkmal für die bereits angedeutete zusammengehörigkeit von Arc. S und Ch kann das fehlen der strophen 17 und 18 angeführt werden, dazu kommen als weiterer beweis noch eine grosse zahl von gemeinsamen lesarten:

2) grene rede and white] rede quhite grene aricht; 4) the[2]] his; 12) also] f.; 15) for to] to; 24) agon] allgone; 25) morowenyng] dawing; 36) forth I gan] comm I forth; 44) on] in; 44) the] f.; 59 u. 85) so[2]] f.; 67) ledres high] hye cidrice; 69 u. 645) to] vnto; 78) golde] like golde; 80) the] was the; 82) sute] nowmer; 91) That] For; 92) lyche] liche to; 112) I] f.; 132) also] was he also; 136) hote] grete; 138) constreynt Arc. S, Ch] die übrig. texte constreynyng; 162) ther] both; 167) awhaped and amate] he wept and was mate; 174) to yow so] his wordis ryght; 178) O Nyobe] O eyen two; 178) thi] yowe; 182) write] write eke; 189) Cause] The cause; 189) al such] suich a; 191) knowyng] knowelage; 195) what] bot; 196) But] Ryght; 199) when] quhen þat; 202) Or] Off; 205) love] louyng; 207) that] or; 208) Sle] To sle; 215) Compleynyng] Compleyne; 232 u. 233) now[2]] and; 234) now[2]] now hote; 238) greuouse] greuance; 239) disdeyn] distresse; 241 u. 322) euer] f.; 241) besy peyn] besynessc; 242) and] and to; 246) in trouth I] I treuth; 253) to] f.; 259) Trouthe] throw I; 266) And Falsnes now his place] And his place now falsnes; 268) the] f.; 282) ne a worde] now inward; 283 u. 408) or] nor; 289) bounde] ybound; 291) thro-girt] onergirt; 294) abide] to habyde; 294) alonge] longer 294, 405, 631) the] thy; 307) Falshed wrongfully] wrongfully falshed; 310) his hest] my behest; 347) of him hist] can of him; 352) Be-set] Yset; 353) that] that ʒit; 357) he] ʒit he; 361) thro] with; 361) bowe] owne bowe; 373) Colkos] Kokes; 383) allas and that] allace in that Ch, in that allace Arc. S; 392) comfort] nor comfort; 394) So] A; 403) men] f.; 407, 410, 412, 415) ne] nor; 408) or] nor; 414) nother in se ne] in se nor on (a. Ch); 419) of] in; 430) with] in; 433) another] they ought; 446) throgh] for; 447) ʒit nur in Arc. S, Ch; 452) feythfully] most feythfully; 458) is] in; 462) by wenyng] as he wend; 476) to] for to; 477) euenly] Arc. S, Ch] die übrigen hs. euen; 479) grace mercie] mercy grace; 483) wounde] wo; 505) also] f.; 510) now] f.; 510) her] his; 527) to helpen] f.; 529) in] all in; 537) ech] ilke; 546) my] by my; 550) vengeaunce] greuance; 552) Hit sitte me not] ʒit shall I nat; 553) But at] Quhereso; 553] wilfully to dye] to do me lyve or dye; 589) be-cause] the cause; 611) Fer in] Into Ch, Vnto Arc. S; 618) thus to her] to hir thus; 619) to] the; 622 u. 645) when] quhen þat; 633) on] of; 639) glade] goodly; 643) now go] go now; 647) werry wery] verily; 666) hit] f.; 670) long hath be] hath long ben; 675) my] to my.

Trotz dieser weitgehenden übereinstimmung ist jedoch keiner der beiden texte von dem andern abhängig, Arc. S nicht von Ch, da Arc. S 1472 und Ch 1508 entstanden, Ch nicht von Arc. S, da Ch in einer reihe von fällen, wo Arc. S abweicht, die richtige lesart bietet:

14) to take] to go take Arc. S; 22) I[2]] þat I; 42) in to (in till Ch)] within; 48) wrest] brest; 56) hote] hote is; 69 u. 70) Her] His; 81) lustely]

full lustily; 90) of deth] of cruell deth; 99) this] this ilke; 107) I] þat I;
110) down] adoun; 136) accesse] excesse; 153) what] quhat þat; 187)
who] quhoso; 200) compleyn] compleynyng; 214) his] his grete; 220) rent]
all rent; 225) grounde] bounde; 229) ys] ben; 248) to] for to; 285) clepe]
cleke; 287) mordred] murder; 303) yf] if þat; 330) of] of him; 360)
fresshe nur in Arc. S; 363) for her love] he for hir; 367) or] eke or;
373) at] to; 374) rote] the rute; 391) worthy nur in Arc. S; trewe
nur in Arc. S; 426) pitouse] double; 429) and] and false; 455) I] þat
I now; 489) shopen] haue shapen; 499) wite] and witt; 527) case] wofull
case; 538) her] ȝow; 573) her] it; 575) sike] to sike; 579) reyn] to
reyne; 586) abide] byde; 599) pleynt] compleynt; 609) axe] ask ȝow;
626) laughe] for to laugh; 640) grace] hir grace; 644) thou] þat thou;
648 u. 659) thus] ryght thus; 652) may] may now; 660) togedre] with
othir; 669) Your] That ȝour; 672) by my trouth] trewily; 673) to] for
to; 676) for] for þat.

Wenn wir nun die in den vorausgehenden paragraphen
gewonnenen resultate zusammenstellen, so erhalten wir für
die hs. und drucke der *Complaint of the Bl. Kn.* folgenden
stammbaum.

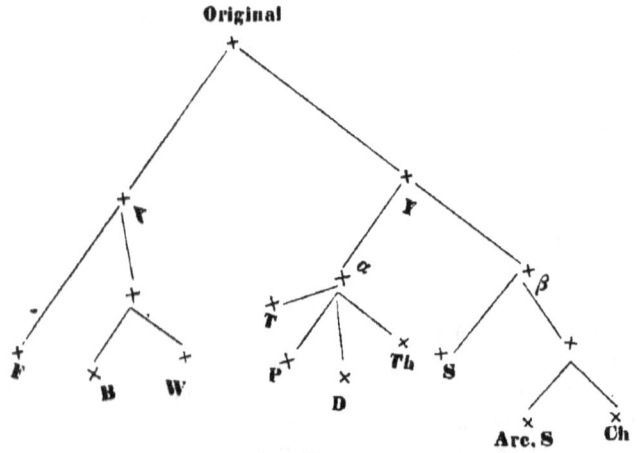

Kapitel III.
Die herstellung des textes.

Von den beiden gruppen X und Y verdient Y als ganzes
genommen den vorzug vor X, wie aus § 1 des vorigen kapitels
hervorgeht, wo von den angeführten lesarten Y in der mehrzahl der fälle den richtigen text bewahrt hat. Dennoch habe
ich mich entschlossen, als grundlage dieser ausgabe eine handschrift aus der gruppe X, nämlich F, zu nehmen, da F den

weitaus besten text vor allen übrigen hs. bietet. Selbst T, welches den am reinsten erhaltenen text in der gruppe Y aufweist, hat sowohl durch verschulden des schreibers von (T, P, D, Th) als auch durch eigenes versehen eine ziemliche anzahl von fehlern, so dass T der hs. F entschieden nachsteht.

Was nun die herstellung des textes anbelangt, so habe ich die fehler und lücken in F auf grund der übrigen hs. verbessert und ausgefüllt; ich wandte sternchen an, wo F eine andere als die erforderliche lesart hatte, und klammern, wo ausgelassene worte, silben oder buchstaben zu ersetzen waren.

Die orthographie von F habe ich stets beibehalten, und nur in der schreibung von eigennamen und allegorischen figuren eine grössere regelmässigkeit durchgeführt, als dies in der hs. geschehen ist. Die anfangsbuchstaben der verse habe ich stets gross geschrieben; die in der hs. häufig zusammengezogenen worte getrennt, oder zusammengehörende bestandteile eines wortes zusammengezogen. Die abkürzungen der hs. habe ich aufgelöst und durch kursiven druck deutlich gemacht; die zahlreichen schnörkel am wortende, wo sie nicht ein durch das metrum erforderliches end-*e* oder ein *n* bedeuten, dagegen unbeachtet gelassen. In allen diesen punkten habe ich die schreibung geregelt, ohne die änderung in den varianten anzugeben. Was die varianten betrifft, so habe ich alle sinnvarianten angegeben. Orthographische varianten habe ich nur selten berücksichtigt; stehen daher bei einer lesart mehrere handschriftzeichen, so gilt das erste zeichen für die schreibung des wortes.

Kapitel IV.
Der versbau.

Ueber den versbau Lydgate's im allgemeinen wie im besonderen haben Schipper im I. bd. seiner englischen Metrik § 196 und Schick a. a. o. p. LIV ff. ausführlich gehandelt, worauf ich ganz besonders verweisen möchte.

Die *Complaint of the Black Knight* ist in fünftaktigen jambischen versen geschrieben, welche zu siebenzeiligen strophen durch die reimfolge *ab ab bcc* verbunden sind. In den beiden schlussstrophen, dem Envoy, ist die rhyme-royal-strophe zur ballad-royal erweitert, mit der gliederung *ab ab bc bc*, — eine art der strophentechnik, wie sie Lydgate in seinem *Guy of*

Warwick und in seinem Chaucer's *January and May* nach-
geahmten gedichte: *Decembre and July* anwandte (vgl. Lydgate's Minor Poems, ed. by Halliwell, Percy Society no. 2).

Bei der untersuchung des metrums fand ich es am vor-
teilhaftesten, die durch Schick (a. a. o. p. XVII) aufgestellten
fünf typen zu grunde zu legen, in die sich sämtliche verse
ohne schwierigkeit einreihen lassen. Natürlich gilt auch hier,
dass viele verse, je nach elision von end-*e* oder nach betonung
verschiedener worte, bald nach dem einen bald nach dem
andern typus gelesen werden können, eine unsicherheit in der
behandlung der rhythmischen gangart der verse, wie sie bei
allen „doggerel-poets, who have not a sensitive ear for rythm"
(Schick) häufig genug vorkommt.

Typus A, vertreten durch regelmässig gebaute fünftak-
tige jamben, findet sich sehr zahlreich in der *Complaint*.
Sämtliche verse, die unter den übrigen vier typen nicht aufgezählt sind, müssen oder können am besten nach diesem typus
gelesen werden.

2) The sóyle hath clá…d ‖ in gréne réde and whíte. — 3) And Phébus
gán ‖ to shéde his strémes shéne. — 8) And hértys hény ‖ fór to récom-
fórte.

Typus B, vertreten durch verse mit epischer caesur, —
eine versart, welche sich in der romanischen poesie grosser
beliebtheit erfreute, und auch in der englischen poesie, bei
Chaucer und seinen nachfolgern und später bei den drama-
tikern des elisabethanischen zeitalters häufig vórkommt.

1) In Máy when Flóra ‖ the frésshe lústy quéne. — 7) To býdde
lóuers ‖ out óf her slépe awáke. — 308) And troúthe ayénwarde ‖ of fál-
shed béreth the bláme. — Weitere verse sind: 114, 141, 147, 196, 244,
258, 274, 351, 366, 408, 418, 419, 422, 433, 445, 488, 516, 524, 527, 536,
607, 619, 627, 628, 647.

Ausser diesen beispielen liesse sich noch eine menge weiterer anführen, in denen unbetontes *e* vor der caesur steht.
Hier wird wohl in der mehrzahl der fälle das end-*e* zu gunsten des rhythmus elidiert resp. apokopiert worden sein, denn
man fühlt sich doch immer unsanft aus dem takte gebracht,
wenn man nach einer reihe von regulär verlaufenden versen
plötzlich solchen mit epischer caesur begegnet.

Typus C, vertreten durch verse mit fehlender senkung
in der caesur. „Diese dem natürlichen flusse des rhythmus

doch eher nachteilige als förderliche eigentümlichkeit" (Schipper) wurde besonders durch Lydgate und in geringerem masse auch durch Lydgate's schüler Stephen Hawes zur anwendung gebracht. Die entstehung solcher verse darf man wohl in gleichem masse dem einfluss der auftaktlosen verse und dem allmählichen weitergreifen des verstummens von end-*e* zuschreiben.

35) That dówn to hém ‖ cást his bémes clére. — 81) That thére vpón ‖ lústelý gan sprýnge. — 140) Hyt wás a déth ‖ fór to hére him gróne. — 356) Agénes whóm ‖ hélpe máy no strífe. — Weitere beispiele sind: 61, 67, 72, 100, 107, 108, 127, 172, 181, 185, 187, 210, 213, 214, 215, 217, 234, 248, 252, 253, 265, 267, 277, 284, 286, 310, 326, 334, 336, 353, 361, 374, 375, 386, 394, 397, 400, 407, 415, 427, 439, 441, 447, 467, 468, 474, 486, 489, 502, 512, 529, 530, 561, 563, 565, 579, 603, 605, 620, 626, 635, 669, 671, 676.

Typus D, vertreten durch verse mit fehlenden auftakt, ein typus, der sich auch bei Chaucer, wenn auch nicht gerade häufig, vorfindet.

99) Bút this wélle ‖ thát I hér rehérse. — 198) Séy ryght nóght ‖ as ín conclúsióun. — 377) Hád in lóve ‖ her lúst and ál her wílle. — Weitere beispiele sind: 14, 65, 96, 98, 101, 114, 142, 189, 258, 319, 320, 333, 338, 342, 367, 368, 408, 409, 415, 419, 422, 431, 462, 466, 471, 544, 560, 600, 612, 621, 644, 645, 662, 665, 673, 675.

Typus E, vertreten durch verse mit doppeltem auftakt:

241) Thĭs is thĕ cólde that éuer dóth his bésy péyn. — 322) Ṽntŏ mý behést yet Ĭ will éuer obéy.

Dieser vers lässt sich leicht durch änderung von *Vnto* in *To*, wie es Shirley gethan, oder durch die annahme von *hest* statt *behest* nach typus A lesen.

In einigen fällen müssen schon im original lücken vorhanden gewesen sein, was wir daraus schliessen können, dass einige verse in den meisten der überlieferten texte statt fünf nur vier takte zählen, was dann einigen schreibern zu ergänzungsversuchen veranlassung gab. Ob die schuld an diesen lücken Lydgate zuzuschreiben ist, wage ich nicht zu entscheiden, da von seinen gedichten bis jetzt nur wenige in textkritischen ausgaben vorhanden sind, und ich also nicht nachprüfen konnte, ob sich noch in anderen fünftaktigen gedichten verse mit vier takten belegen lassen. Vielleicht trifft die schuld auch den schreiber, welche ja, wie wir aus Chaucer's berühmter klage an Adam Scryvein wissen, an sorgfalt oft sehr viel zu wünschen übrig gelassen haben.

Vers 355 lesen alle mit einer ausnahme: *For him set last upon a daunce.* Hier fehlt vor *him* — *he*, das Shirley richtig conjiciert hat. Die lücke ist wahrscheinlich durch zusammenschreiben der beiden mit gleichen buchstaben beginnenden worte entstanden.

Aehnlich wird es sich auch mit vers 477 verhalten, wo auf rechnung von *by* das fehlen der endung *ly* zu setzen sein wird: *Thus fareth hit now even[ly] by me.* In diesem falle hat dann (Arc. S, Ch) richtig ergänzt.

In vers 360: *Unto the hert with Venus sight* haben Arc. S und S ergänzungen versucht, wovon die lesart von Arc. S: *fresshe Venus* vor der von S: *goddes Venus* den vorzug verdient.

Dem vers 379 giebt S durch einsetzung von *loo* die richtige länge: *Of Thetes eke [loo] the fals Arcite.*

Vers 391: *Wher Mars her knight and her man* erweitert S zu: *Wher Mars her knight and hir owen man*; Arc. S dagegen: *Wher Mars the worthy knight, hir trwe man,* das gar keine üble conjektur ist.

In den versen 357 und 447 wird als lückenbüsser von dem schreiber von (Arc S, Ch) ȝit eingesetzt:

357) For al his trouthe [ȝit] he lost his lyfe. — 447) And most of all [ȝit] I me compleyn.

Diese von den einzelnen schreibern gemachten conjekturen habe ich in dem texte beibehalten, obwohl ich gerne zugebe, dass man in die richtigkeit derselben zweifel setzen kann.

In der behandlung der c a e s u r zeigt Lydgate grosse eintönigkeit; mit einer beinahe constanten regelmässigkeit lässt er die caesar nach dem zweiten takte eintreten, und nur in wenigen fällen lässt sich eine abweichung von dieser regel belegen, abweichungen, die wohl eher dem zufall als bewusster absicht ihr entstehen verdanken.

So haben wir caesur nach dem **3.** takte:

89) Wher só couértelý ‖ he díd[e] hýde. — 131) In bláke and white cólour, ‖ pále and wán.

Wohl eher **v e r m i s c h t e   c a e s u r** als caesur nach dem **1.** takte ist in den folgenden versen anzunehmen:

88) Isláyn was ‖ thró vengeáunce óf Cupíde. — 421) But lésinges ‖ with her fálse fláterýe.

Was die c a e s u r a r t e n anbelangt, so findet sich ein ententschiedenes übergewicht der gewöhnlichen caesur über die beiden anderen arten, epische und lyrische caesur. Schipper's behauptung, dass in Lydgate's strophischen gedichten die epische caesur häufiger vorkomme als die lyrische (Engl. Metrik I, s. 497), die ich auch bei der lektüre anderer gedichte Lydgate's bestätigt fand, trifft in der *Compl. of the Bl. Kn.* nicht zu, denn es finden sich in den ersten 200 versen nur halb so viel epische als lyrische caesuren.

Taktumstellungen, einerseits durch die natürliche betonung des wortes, andererseits auch durch rhetorische absicht hervorgerufen, finden sich sowohl am anfang des verses als auch nach der caesur.

I. Zu anfang des verses: 13) Bàd in dispíte; 45) Lỳke as it shólde; 49) Rỳght as her hért; 119) Fòrth in the párke; 167) Grùffe on the gróunde; 168) Sòle by himsélf; 175) Lỳch as he sáyde; 224) Pàrcel declàre; 240) Còlde of dyspíte; 274) Fàlsly accúsed; 334) Lòve unto hím; 420) Àl ys for nòghte; 507) Chèfe of counséyle; 587) Sòle to compléyn.

II. Nach der caesur: 42) wàlled with gréne stoón; 83) clòsyng the wélle; 224) gròunde of my péynes; 588) ùnder the bówes grene.

Doppelte senkung lässt sich einige mal belegen:

85) hólsŏm ănd sŏ vértuoús; 332) and óf his péyne nŏ rĕlése; 623) vnvisíblĕ yŏu boúnde.

Silbenverschleifung resp. Synkope findet sich ziemlich häufig:

46) sheuer in pecis; 74) mony a tre; 291) Euen at the deth; 295) Consîder and se; 528) euere in oon; usw.

In der behandlung des Hiatus nimmt Lydgate eine sonderstellung gegen Chaucer ein. Während bei letzterem nur in wenigen fällen nach *th* und vor *h* Hiatus stattfindet (s. ten Brink S. V. § 270), sonst aber das zusammentreffen eines unbetonten auslautenden *e* mit folgendem vokal-anlaut sorgfältig vermieden wird, lässt der erstere den Hiatus mehrmals zu:

80) sóftĕ ás velúet (dieser Hiatus wurde von dem schreiber von (Arc. S, Ch) getilgt vgl. varianten); 88) vengeaúncĕ of Cupíde; 238) cáusĕ eúery déle; 266) plácĕ óccupíeth.

Die alliteration kommt ziemlich häufig vor, besonders wendet der dichter sie an, wenn er eine lebhaftere sprache führt, wie bei naturschilderungen oder bei intensiveren gefühlsäusserungen, besonders bemerkenswert ist in dieser hinsicht strophe 3. Sehr oft mag jedoch die alliteration durch blossen zufall entstanden sein.

4) Amyd the *B*ole with al the *b*emes *b*ryght; 60) That smale *b*uddes
and rounde *b*lomes lyte; 70) Vnto her *k*nyght i*c*alled Demophone; 234)
Now colde as ise now as *c*oles rede; 321) And by her mouthe *d*amned
that I shal *d*eye; 521) Yet of my *d*ethe let this bé the *d*ate; 55) From
al assaute of *P*hebus *f*eruent *f*ere; 315) Ne *f*ayleth not to *f*ynde grace
and spede; 11) A*g*eyn the *g*oodly *g*lade *g*reye morowe; 84) And al the
erbes *g*roving on the *g*rounde; 8) And *h*ertys *h*euy for to recomforte;
9) From drery*h*ed of *h*euy nyghtis sorowe; 109) My bitter *l*angour yf
hyt myght a*l*ay; 219) The peynful *l*yve the body *l*angwysshing; 312) Shal
for his *m*ede fynde *m*ost offence; 333) Not — withstondyng his *m*anhode
and his *m*yght; 13) Bad in dis*p*ite of Daunger and Dis*p*eyre; 92) Ne
lyche the *p*itte of the *P*egace; 3) And Phebus gan to s*h*ede his stremes
s*h*ene; 185) To sorow also sighing and wepyng; 74) And *m*ony a *t*re
*m*o then I can *t*elle; 665) Werred *T*routhe with his *t*iranye; 593) Were
in the *w*aves of the *w*ater fall usw.

Kapitel V.

Reime.

In bezug auf dauer und klang der reimvokale befolgt
Lydgate zum grössten teil dieselben gesetze wie Chaucer.
Nur in einigen punkten weicht er von dem sprachgebrauch
Chaucer's ab; es sind dies die vermischung von offenen und
geschlossenen *e* und *o* reimen, die assonanzen, und die reim-
verbindungen von y : ye, und kons. : kons. + e.

Quellen des ę sind für unseren text:

1) *ae. ǽ*: (umlaut aus ai) spręde 32, bręde 33, lęde 177; dęle 238;
clęne 126; hęte 28, 230, swęte (ae. swǽtan) 231; — ws. ǽ (germ. â)
męde 30; bręthe 294, 566 (diese beiden worte haben neutrales e, das hier,
weil mit offenem ę reimend, offene aussprache hatte; vgl. ten Brink SV
§ 25. Kluge in Pl. Grdriss I, s. 891).

2) *ae. ĕ*, das in offener silbe gelängt wird: spęke 282, 660, wręke
284, 663, bręke 662.

3) *ae. ēā*: dęde 232, ręde 234, 596; giltelęs 272, perelęs 346, chęs
(ae. cēās) 395; dęthe 293, 567.

4) *afrz. ai*, das vor dentalen zu ę monophthongiert wird: pęs 273,
relęse 332.

5) *griech.-lat. e*: Palamidęs 330, Erculęs 344, Ipomonęs 393.

Quellen des ẹ sind:

1) *ae. ē*: mẹ 455, 477, 543, 547, 603, shẹ 549; sẹche 474; blẹde 180,
363, spẹde 315, v. 598, hẹde (ne. heed) 327, 364; wẹl (ae. wêl vgl. Pl.
Grdr. s. 879) 113; fẹle 115, 237; quẹne 1, 516, 674, shẹne 3, grẹne 125,
515, 588, kẹne 513, 587; — hierher gehören auch die beispiele, in denen
me. ẹ auf angl.-kent. ê = ws. îe, ŷ, zurückgehrt: hẹre 193, 217, nẹde
179; fẹre 55 (für ŷ, umlaut aus u) (hier hat auch das angl. ŷ vgl. Cook's
Glossary zu den Lindisfarne Gospels); — ferner beispiele, in denen me. ê

auf angl. ê = ws. ǽ (germ. â, got. ê) zurückgeht: wręche (ae. wrǽc)
471, lęche 473; ręde 324, dręde 563; auch die composita mit -hede (ê <
umgelaut. ǽ) (vgl. Pl. Grdr. s. 874) darf man hierher gruppieren. lou-
lyhęde 314, falshęde 326, womanhęde 525, 561.

2) *ae.* *ēo*: bę 142, 256, 506, 605, bęn 281, sę 144, 445, 541, 619,
sęn 283, 676, flę 509, frę 544, knę 617, dęre 435.

3) *afrz. e aus lat. a*: pite 145, 443, 479, 508, cruelte 254, 446, enemyte 257, deyte 454, clęre 35, 56, 614, chęre 216, 437, 613, appęr 611.

4) *afrz. ie*, das im aglon. monophthongiert wird: matęr 191; re-
lęve 614.

Im allgemeinen hält nun Lydgate die offenen und geschlossenen *e*-reime ziemlich genau auseinander; in den folgenden fällen hat er jedoch diese scheidung unterlassen:

suęte; hęte 27; gręne : clęne 125 (ebenso z. b. in Pur le Roy s. 16,
Chorl & Bird s. 181, Secreta Secretorum v. 1374); lęde : nęde : blęde 177;
fęle : dęle 237; ręde (ae. rēad) : spęde 596.

Pflichten wir ten Brink's auffassung bei, nach dessen ansicht (S. V. § 25, 2) lęde & clęne auch mit geschlossenem ę vorkommen, so wären die betreffenden reime bei Lydgate nicht
absolut unrein.

In bezug auf die *o*-reime kommen solche reime wie stǫọd :
abǫde (ae. abâd), oder wode (ae. wôd) : abrǫde (s. Schick a. a. o.
p. LX) in der *Compl.* nicht vor. Eine vermischung beider
quantitäten könnte man annehmen in: wǫo : alsǫ : to 149, alsǫ :
do 160, 559, alsǫ : therto 419. In diesen beispielen geht ǫ
auf ae. â mit vorausgehendem *w* zurück. Nun hat dieses me. ǫ
die entschiedene tendenz, im laufe der me. zeit sich der geschlossenen aussprache zu nähern, ein vorgang, der bei Chaucer
(vgl. ten Brink S. V. § 31 und Bowen Engl. St. XX 431 ff.)
schon eingetreten ist, so dass wir obige reime nicht als un-
reine sondern als vollkommen jener zeit entsprechende be-
trachten müssen.

Assonanzen: In der *Compl.* haben wir vier fälle von
assonanzen, eine zahl, die im verhältnis zu der einen assonanz
Chaucers in Troil II 884 syke : endyte : whyte für unser gedicht als ungenauigkeit schwer ins gewicht fällt.

white : bryght : nyght 2, solche verbindungeu, die auf eine allmäh-
liche verflüchtigung des spiranten hinweisen, kommen vereinzelt in me.
zeit vor (vgl. Kluge in Pl. Grdr. I. S. 849). Für Chaucer giht ten Brink
S V § 121 einen beleg an : plit (plight) : appetit; im Frgmt B des Rosenroman's 2555 findet sich dighte : delyt; bei Lydgate's fortsetzer der Secreta Secretorum, Burgh, stossen wir verschiedene male auf solche
bindungen, z. b.: light : vomit 1615; wyght : Appetit 1904; delit : right :

Appetit 2231; whyte : right 2590; bedeutende fortschritte hat die verflüchtigung im Court of Love gemacht, welch gedicht nach Skeat
(Prioress Tale p. LXXXI) c. 1500 geschrieben ist und wo sich mehrere
solher — it: iχt bindungen finden z. b. write : aright 13, delite : hight
144 : sight 452 : knyghte 870 : brighte : white 790.

Die weiteren assonanzen sind: for-iuged · excused 274 (schon von
ten Brink Chaucer-Studien s. 171 und von Skeat Academy 10. Aug. 1878
s. 144 angeführt) speke : wreke : cepe 282 (ebenfalls von Skeat ange-
merkt) blynde . wenyng 461.

Die ungehörigkeit dieser reime wurde von einzelnen schreibern gemerkt, und infolgedessen durch mehr oder minder ge-
lungene änderungen zu tilgen versucht, vgl. varianten.

Vollkommen abweichend vom Chaucer'schen sprachgebrauch sind die bindungen y : ye, worauf ten Brink in seinen
Chaucer-Studien s. 22 ff. zum ersten male aufmerksam gemacht hat. Während sich in sämtlichen gedichten Chaucer's
nicht ein einziger reim von y : ye vorfindet, kommen solche
reime in Lydgate's gedichten öfters vor. Die *Compl. of the
Bl. Kn.* weist deren drei auf: greuosly : petously : maladye 135,
felyngly : maladye 188, why : feythfully : I crie 450.

Eine ähnliche vernachlässigung des end-*e* liegt in den
folgenden reimen vor: assaye inf. : allaye inf. : I lay prt. 107,
may : paye : day 534.

Reime von *Kons.* : *Kons.* + *e* sind: bryghte : nyght 4; wel : fele
inf. 113; entente : present 209; ageyn · tweyne : peyne 233; mente prt.
: diligent 246; sovereyn : cheyn 288; Palamides : relese 330, cas : grace
: allas 527 (der reim s : ce findet sich auch bei Chaucer im Sir Thopas,
wo er bekanntlich zur verspottung der bänkelsängerweise seine sonst
streng eingehaltenen reimregeln einige mal überschreitet (vgl. ten Brink
S. V. § 223 β). I assente : commaundement : testament 558; seyn : peyne
570; myn : enclyne : declyne 639; wente prt. : entente : shent pp. 646;
peyne ageyn 650; quene : seen 674.

Lydgate's reimbehandlung zeigt also im vergleich mit
Chaucer schon einen ziemlichen fortschritt in der abstossung
des auslautenden *e*. Ausführlicher wird darüber im nächsten
kapitel gehandelt werden.

Sogenannte „cheap rimes" (Suffixalreime auf -aunce, -é, -ence, -hede,
-oun) finden sich in der *Compl.* häufig.

Von doppelformen finden sich: dyeth : occupieth 265, dagegen abreyde : deyde 15, deye : obeye 321.

Von reimkünsten, wie reicher, gebrochener, leoninischer,
intermittierender reim, die sich in Chaucer's werken so häufig
finden, und ihnen eine grössere mannigfaltigkeit verleihen,

macht Lydgate nur sehr spärlichen, zum teil auch gar keinen
gebrauch.

Reiche reime: goon : agoon 22, 136, noon : oon 526, anone : every-
chone 174; lyte : delyte 60; lay : alay 106; debate : abate 242; serue ·
deserue 247, founde : confounde 480, 634; recommaunde : commaunde :
demaunde 562; reporte : dysporte 60l; enclyne : declyne 641; adovne adv. :
Adoun 643.

Leoninische reime: assay : alay 107; avayle travayle 412.

Kapitel VI.

Zur behandlung des end-*e*.

Bei der untersuchung über die behandlung des end-*e* habe
ich mein hauptaugenmerk auf diejenigen fälle gerichtet, welche
sich inmitten der vershälften befinden, sich also durch den
rhythmus ziemlich genau bestimmen lassen. In den fällen, wo
das end-*e* vor der caesur steht, ist es bei Lydate wegen der
existenz des typus C etwas schwierig, angaben über den silbenwert des *e* zu machen. Ich habe daher dem vorgange Schick's
folgend solche fälle nicht berücksichtigt, und es auch unterlassen im texte ein *e* hinzuzufügen, selbst wo ich glaubte,
dass Lydgate es gesprochen haben würde.

§ 1. Substantiva. Vokalische stämme.
Starke masculina und neutra.

Nom. und accus.: Entsprechend dem ae. konsonant. aus-
laut (mit ausnahme der kurzsilbigen *i*- und *u*-stämme) findet
sich auch im me. keine endung. Ob wir in dem acc. wey
(: costeye inf. 38) ein unorgan. *e* ansetzen dürfen, wie es Orrm
(vgl. Sachse, das unorgan. *e* im Orrmulum s. 7) und Chaucer
(vgl. ten Brink S. V. § 199₅) thun, ist wahrscheinlich, da Lydgate es auch in seinem *Temple of Glas* mitten im verse thut
(vgl. Schick a. a. o. p. LXV), ebenso auch in seinem *Guy of
Warwick* str. 37.₇ und 53.₃ (Ausgabe von Zupitza. Wiener
Sitzungsberichte Bd. 74), ist jedoch hier mit sicherheit nicht
zu entscheiden.

Genitiv endet auf -*es*, entsprechend der ae. endung
lyvës 483, 316.

Dativ. Wie schon bei Orrm, so ist in der folgezeit auch
bei Chaucer und Lydgate in den meisten fällen der dativ gleich
dem nom. In der *Compl.* sind nur wenige beispiele vorhanden,

in denen sich das alte dativ-*e* erhalten hat, z. b. beddë 646,
gatë 40. Dieses wort findet sich schon bei Orrm (vgl. Sachse
a. a. o. § 25) im singular mit einem unorgan. *e*, wo es Sachse
nach dem vorgange von Zupitza als analogiebildung nach den
kurzsilbigen femininen erklärt, hervorgerufen durch die gleich-
heit der pluralendung -*u*. Im vorliegenden falle können wir
vielleicht auch compromissbildung zwischen ae. geat und an.
gata annehmen, zumal da die erhaltung des gutturals auf
skandinav. beeinflussung hinweist und die beiden wörter auch
begrifflich nicht weit auseinanderliegen.

Plural: es < as; diese endung des mascul. wurde auch
auf andere stämme und Genera übertragen: strëmes 3, 77, 592;
bemës 4, 35, 614; briddës 23, 43; houndës 97; holtys 119;
treës 123; wordïs 170, 513; terës 178, 579; sighës 218; colës
234; armës 658, — Synkope des *e* im einsilbigen wort findet
sich bei leves 33, dagegen findet stets synkope statt bei mehrsilbigen paroxytonis : louers 7, 371, 653, in v. 400 verlangt
der rhythmus des verses die betonung louérs, eine betonung,
die sich auch bei Gower in der *Confessio Amantis* oft genug
belegen lässt (vgl. Child's *Observations on the language of
Chaucer and Gower* in Ellis O. E. E. P. I. 369).

Ia- resp. *u*-stämme weisen als vertreter eines ae. *e*
resp. *u* am ende silbebildendes *e* auf: lechë (ae. angl. lêce) 481,
wodë (ae. wudu) 45.

Starke feminina.

Nom. endet auf *e*, das sich bei den ursprüngl. kurzsilbigen
substantiven als abschwächung des ae. *u*, bei den langsilbigen
als analoge neubildung nach den obliquen casus einstellt.
Trouthë (ae. trêowð) 259; talë (ae. talu) 260; love (ae. lufu)
327, mit stummem e Love 420.

Genitiv endet nach analogie der masculina auf -*es*.
Trouthës 267, 272; lovës 290.

Dativ und accus. enden auf -*e*. sorowë 17, 404, 632,
(mit apokopiertem *e* in 415); lovë 49, 413; shadowë 83; trouthë
159, 264, 269, 288, 289, 311, 620; arowë 464; hestë 571;
shamë 626.

Plural hat die endung -*es*: bankys 79; woundës 133;
talës 423, 511; rowës 596; bei mehrsilbigen trat synkope des

e ein: lesyngẹs 421. Einen alten dativ-plural habeu wir in dem zum zeitadverb gewordenen whilom 296.

Konsonantische stämme.

-*n*-stämme.

Mascul.: die endung des nom. ist *e* als fortsetzung des ae. -*a*: wellë 83.

Plural endet analog nach den st. subst. auf -*es*. blosmës 58; blomës 60; bowys 53, 69, 588; namës 124; — die alte pluralendung auf -*n* hat sich erhalten in fon 280 : anon.

Femin.: nom., dat. und acc. enden auf -*e*: erthë 69, 359; hertë 220, 363, 662.

Pluralendung ist -*es*: hertys 8, 405, 602; asshës 222, 232; tongës 255; einen alten plural auf -*n* haben wir in flon 468 (: gon). Analog nach den -*n*-stämmen wurde öfters der plural der -*r*-stämme gebildet (vgl. ten Brink S. V. § 215) sustren 488.

Neutra: singul. erë 152; **plural** auf -*n* eyen 223, 579.

Weitere konsonant. stämme sind: **genit.**: nyghtis 9; mannys 182 (plural: men).

Französ. substantiva.

Die substantiva franz. ursprungs behalten in der überwiegenden mehrzahl der fälle entsprechend dem afrz. ihr silbebildendes *e* bei: Naturë 10; bawmë 27; vengeauncë 88; stilë 177; placë 167, 266; causë 238, 450; jugë 283; fraudë 426; gracë 445, 640; prudencë 499; arkë 590. — Apokope des tonlosen -*e* findet statt in peynẹ 332; cherẹ 500.

Die endung des plurals ist *es*: pesis 46; flourës 53, 127; nymphës 95; hurtis 133; peynës 224, 587; armës 410; sawtës 418.

Bei Paroxytonis tritt jedoch synkope des unbetonten *e* ein: tapitẹs 51; póetys 93; colours 126; pilers 348, 351; seruantịs 401.

§ 2. Adiectiva.

Singular: Entsprechend der ae. form haben die **stark flectierten** adiectiva keine endung; nur die **ja-stämme** weisen, wie schon im ae., tonloses *e* auf: grenë 2, 65; trwë 244, 408; stilë 409. — Die **schwach** flectierten adiectiva haben als vertreter der vollen ae. endungen tonloses *e*. Das schwache adiectiv steht:

I. Nach dem bestimmten artikel: fresshë 2, 71; gladë, greyë 11; grenë 30, 387; smothë 57; yongë 80; hardë 244, 440; trwë 325, 331; whichë (als adiect.) 298, 435; foulë 390; brightë 485, 612; samë 624; — ohne endung jedoch the ful 268.

II. Nach einem demonstrativpronomen: this blyndë 309; this gretë 455 (kann auch mit apokop. *e* gelesen werden, wenn man doppelten auftakt nicht annehmen will), this coldë 515; this echë samë 537.

III. Nach einem possessivpronomen: my fullë 297, 317, 542; her falsë 421; her wysë 494; your trwë 669; flexionslos jedoch: his high 366.

IV. Vor einem vokativ: gladë 639; wohl auch feirë 627.

V. Vor personennamen: saintë John 12; yongë Piramus 365; wohl auch trwë Tristram 366 (Typus B); falsë Jasoun 372 (typus A).

Flectionslos sind jedoch in allen diesen fällen die Paroxytona, welche notwendiger weise auslautendes *e* apokopieren: the holsomę 14, 65; his persaunt 28, 591; his woful 172; Thou woful 180; the woful 193, 220, 584; the peynful 219; O ryghtful 269; thy wilful 456.

Im plural endigen sowohl die schwachen als auch die starken adiectiva auf tonloses -*e*. smalë 60; quykë 77; fresshë 133; falsë 207, 384, 403, 469: trwë 208, 469, 638, 649; sharpë 468, 524; bryghtë 592; allë 638, 649, 653; — apokopiert ist das tonlose -*e* in bothe 624 und selbstverständlich in dem Paroxytonon faythful 402.

Die französ. adiectiva haben sowohl in flectierter wie unflectierter form ihr tonloses *e* beibehalten: roundë 60; purë 94; hugë 116; delytablë 122; sobrë 212; feblë 228; straungë 412; doublë 454; benignë 500.

§ 3. Pronomina

weisen mit einer ausnahme dieselben formen auf wie bei Chaucer; durch das metrum verlangt wird die dativform echę 90, welche bei Chaucer echę lautet (vgl. ten Brink S. V. § 255): Einen starken Genitiv Plural haben wir in altherlast 503, 561.

§ 4. Adverbien

enden bei den aus adiectiven gebildeten formen auf tonloses *e*: loudë 45, 262; hotë 56; fastë 121, 598; longë 316; — endungslos ist wohl soote 72. Als fortsetzung voller ae. endungen zeigt sich toulóses *e* in: outë 48; aboutë 82; withoutë 287, 299, 554, 660; besidë 196; byyondë 351; oftë 466; abovë 625; analoges *e* haben: betwyxë 235, 563; ekë 380; — ohne endung sind: while 566, 596; lichę 87, 92; amiddę 4, 387; frz. adv. safę 378, 439, 451; — auf *es* endet: ageynës 159, 242, 253, 356, 672.

Composition.

Tonloses *e* zwischen haupt- und nebenton behält in engl. wie roman. wörtern meist seinen silbenwert bei: sekënes 18, 134 (jedoch sekęnesse 165); hawëthorne (ae. hagaþorn) 71; wodëbynde (ae. wudubind) 129; jugëment 277, 280; avisëment 278; giltëles 272, 450, 514; perëles 346; lustëly 81, 611; couertëly 89; verëly 115; priuëly 147; hastëly 523; — diesen fällen gegenüber haben wir jedoch dedęly 132, 149, 222; hertly 139, softly 146; falsly 274; namęly 480; sothęly 536; faręwel 653.

§ 5. Verbum.

Da Lydgate in der bildung der starken und schwachen verben vollständig mit Chaucer übereinstimmt, so gehe ich im folgenden nicht darauf ein, und untersuche nur die endungen der verben, insofern sie für die behandlung des end-*e* in betracht kommen:

Infinitiv endet auf -*ën* resp. *ë*: byddë 7; rysën 10; refreshë 103; walkën 118; beholdë 128; markë 153; makë 155, 509; rehersën 175; writën 187, 192; knowë 188; fyghtën 242; excusë 282; fyndë 312, 315, 392, 476; thenkën 432; laughën 448; seruë 452; axë 479; helpën 527; dyë 536; ryvë 576; semë 606; descendë 631; hauë 657.

Es finden sich jedoch auch fälle, wo apokope der endung statt hatte: herę 23, 43, 213; ley 211; takę 254; hauę 271 483; savę 406; givę 495; berę 604; makę 606; let 630.

Infinitiv -*n* ist erhalten in: goon : stoon 42; ben : sen 283, seyn : peyn 568.

Praesens Indicat. 1. pers. sgl. endet auf *e*: hauë 191; takë [?] 330; compleynë 455; axë 531, 609; menë 614, 659. Beispiele für apokope der endung sind: lyę 289, 563; byę 435.

2. pers. sgl. endet auf -*est*: seëst 289; — mit synkopiertem endungsvokal: felįst 180

3. pers. sgl. endet auf -*eth*: wepëth 66; accordëth 183; menëth 302; seruëth 313; faylëth 315; furthęrëth 384; causëth

444; markëth 462; shetëth 462; happëth 466; farëth 477; haldëth 510; stondëth 529; sufficëth 539, 547; lastëth 566. Synkope finden wir in: bereth 308; taketh 327; leteth 469; maketh 472; pleseth 666. Contraction der endung haben wir in: sitte 552.

Im plural haben wir die endung -en resp- -e: stiken 438; akë 524; jedoch haue 258, 264. Einen rest der alten pluralbildung auf -th haben wir in goth 329.

Praesens coniunktiv: sgl. lustë 538; pl. bledën 528; — ohne endung: list 523.

Imperativ: Sgl. Im gegensatz zu Chaucer, der in der imperativbildung noch zwischen starken und schwachen verben scheidet, indem die letzteren gemäss dem ae. ein end-e haben, findet sich im vorliegenden gedicht kein solcher unterschied mehr: let 178, 521, 620, 635, 671; do 629; go 674; consider 295; haue 633; shew 633; further 638. Plural. 2. pers.: leyth 603.

Particip praesens endet auf -ing: norysshing 59; closyng 83; grovyng 84, 86; lying 139, 215; wondring 142; compleynyng 215; rennyng 458; abydyng 564; helpyng 630; Preyng 648, 654; hierzu ein anglonorm. adiectivisch gebrauchtes particip persaunt 28, 591, wofür Chaucer piercing setzt.

Verbalnomen endet auf -ing: brynnyng 114, 205; sighing 185; morenyng 186; knowyng 191; menyng 408, 431; ryding 412; shedyng 417; woundyng 418, 470; iupartyng 419; lesynges 421; shetyng 466; gruching 554; vnkynnyng 607; furtheryng 631.

Praeteritum der starken verba: Die 1. und 3. pers. wie bei Chaucer endungslos. 2. pers. auf ë haben wir in thou leyë : preie inf. : deye inf. 620. Im plural haben wir gunnë 32 (daneben auch gan 61); shopën 489; apokopiertes e hat were 597.

Praeteritum der schwachen verba: 2. pers. sgl. endet auf -est: haddest 621, 644. Die übrigen personen enden auf -ed, resp. de, te. Für ëd kein beispiel; synkope trat ein bei loved 316. — Auf -de, -te enden: woldë 22, 49; myghtë 41, 142; didë 89, 363; haddë 143, 145; settë 348; madë 506; wentë 585; keptë 582. (Analog nach kepte u. a. traten zwei ursprünglich stark flectierte verba in die klasse der schwach flectierten über: slepte 93 (slepan wurde schon im ae. vereinzelt schwach flectiert vgl. Sievers, Ags. Grtk. § 394, anm. 2

und § 405) und lepte 96.)   Ohne end-*e* finden sich: woldę 243;
myght 381.

Participia der starken verba enden auf -*en*: bollyn
101; fallën 105; takën 300, 497; rysën 655; ferner slayn (ae.
geslægen) 386, 513; seyn 434 (daneben auch schon seen 437).
Participia der schwachen verba enden auf -*ed*: driëd
29; enclosëd 39; celurëd 52; closëd 64; refresshëd 113; relesëd
116; benchëd 126; prouëd 161; awhapëd 168; hinderëd 206;
styntëd 256; entrëd 267; damnëd 276, 293; admyttëd 281;
professëd 296; feynëd 423, 429; oppressëd 437; mordrëd 513;
mys-reportëd 605; recurëd 651; exilëd 680. — Synkope haben
wir in: góldę-borned 34; destreynęd 134; banysshęd 320; damnęd
321; disposęd 494; welapayęd 549.

Das praefix *I*- ist erhalten in: I-callëd 70; I-slayn 88;
I-furtherëd 327; I-woundëd 361; I-meynt 457; I-passëd 591.

Contrahierte formen sind: clad 2; over-sprad 51;
knytte 290; thro-girt 291; set 352.

Aus diesen beispielen geht wohl mit ziemlicher klarheit
hervor, dass Lydgate in der behandlung des auslautenden *e*
im wesentlichen sich von denselben regeln leiten liess, wie sie
von Chaucer in seinen werken befolgt wurden. In der mehrzahl der angeführten fälle hat das end-*e* seinen silbenwert
beibehalten, und nur in einigen fällen lässt sich ein fortschritt
in der abstossung der endung erkennen, wobei man manchen
fall auch als zu gunsten des metrums geschehen erklären kann,
was ja auch bei Chaucer keineswegs selten ist. Ungewöhnlich
aber ist bei Chaucer die nichtbeachtung des end-*e* im reime,
die sich bei Lydgate ziemlich oft belegen lässt, die aber zum
grössten teil französ. wörter betrifft, woraus hervorgeht, dass
„Lydgate does not always refrain from doing at the end of
a verse, what Chaucer does not hesitate to do in the middle“
(Schick a. a. o. p. LXII).

Kapitel VII.
Zur autorschaft.

Die *Complaint of the Black Knight* wurde seit dem aus-
gange des 15. jahrh. wohl allgemein Chaucer zugeschrieben.
Obwohl Shirley in einem seiner mss. Lydgate ausdrücklich und
an mehreren stellen als autor nennt, so bleiben diese angaben

doch vollkommen unberücksichtigt, vielleicht auch unbekannt.
Der erste, der das gedicht Chaucer namentlich zuschrieb, war,
soweit man bis jetzt ersehen kann, der schreiber der vorlage
zu der schott. hs. Arc. S und zu Chepmann's druck. Thynne
war der erste, der das gedicht in seine gesamtausgabe aufnahm, ob er dazu durch die kenntnis von Chepmann's druck
veranlasst wurde, und es bona fide als Chaucer's erzeugnis
aufnahm, oder ob auch hier zutrifft, was Skeat (M. P.) von
anderen gedichten sagt, dass „he wittingly and purposely chose
to throw into his edition poems, which he knew to have been
written by Lydgate or by Gower" lässt sich nicht entscheiden.
Ihm nachfolgend hat dann Leland in seiner biographie Chaucer's
die *Complaint* als *Querela Equitis cog. Nigri* Chaucer zugeschrieben. Von dieser zeit an bis herunter auf die 60er jahre
dieses jahrhunderts figuriert die *Compl.* in der liste der Chaucer-
schen werke. Der erste, welcher veranlasst durch die reimver-
bindung *y* : *ye* in die echtheit der *Compl.* zweifel setzte und diese
dann auch durch handschriftliche autorität (Shirley's Ms.) geklärt
fand, war der um die Chaucerforschung hochverdiente biblio-
thekar der Cambridger universitätsbibliothek, Mr. H. Bradshaw.
Wie so viele andere entdeckungen publicierte er auch diese nicht,
sondern begnügte sich damit, sie im privatgespräch bekannten
gelehrten mitzuteilen, welche dann für ihre verbreitung sorge
trugen. Von dieser zeit an wurde dann auch die *Complaint*
aus der liste der werke Chaucer's gestrichen und nur noch
unter vorbehalt in die gesamtausgaben aufgenommen. Es sind
aber nicht allein die bindungen *y* : *ye*, welche die unechtheit
ausser zweifel stellen würden, es berechtigen uns auch noch
andere erscheinungen, die *Compl.* Chaucer abzusprechen. Bereits in kapitel V (reime) habe ich darauf hingewiesen, dass
sich in der *Compl.* mehrere ungenaue reime vorfinden, welche
sich der überaus genau reimende Chaucer niemals hätte. zu
schulden kommen lassen. Dies sind besonders die reime von
geschlossen *ẹ* mit offen *ę*, von *Kons.* : *Kons* + *e* und die
assonanzen, auf grund derer jedes gedicht, in dem sich solche
bindungen finden, als unecht bezeichnet werden muss.

Hierzu kommt noch die behandlung des verses, die in
vieler beziehung von der Chaucer's abweicht, insbesondere
dürfte allein schon das häufige vorkommen des typus C ge-
nügen, die *Compl.* Chaucer abzusprechen, und dürfte uns zugleich

eine handhabe geben, das gedicht Lydgate zuzuschreiben, in dessen werken sich der typus C als besondere eigentümlichkeit häufig findet.

Auch das häufige vorkommen von *do* und *did* mit dem infinitiv „as mere auxiliaries instead of being independent verbs with a causal signification" ist nach Lounsbury (Studies in Chaucer I 484, 498—501, II 72—75) eine eigentümlichkeit, die sich in Chaucer's werken nicht findet, und ein beweis der unechtheit. Solche umschreibungen haben wir in der *Compl.*: v. 68, 72, 89, 196, 363, 413, 600.

Die wichtigste stütze, die autorschaft feststellen zu können, hat uns Shirley in seinem Addit. Ms. 16165 geliefert. Wie schon bei der beschreibung der handschrift bemerkt, hat uns Shirley an vier verschiedenen stellen Lydgate als verfasser der *Compl.* angeführt. Dazu kommt noch, dass er in einem prolog, den er seinem ms. voranstellte und worin er den des ms. beschreibt, Lydgate als den verfasser bezeichnet:

þanne and ye wol þe wryting suwe   72
Schul ye fynde wryten of a knyght
þat serued his soueraine lady bright
As done þees louers Amerous
Whos lyff is offt seen parillous
Askeþe of hem þat have hit vsed
A dieux Ioenesse I am refused
Whos complaynt is al in balade
þat Daun Iohan of Bury made   80
Lydegate þe Munk cloþed al in blacke.

Diese stelle wurde von Skeat M. P. p. XLV als beweis für Lydgate's autorschaft der *Compl.* angeführt. Demgegenüber möchte Schick a. a. o. p. LXXXII diese stelle für den *Temple of Glas* gedeutet wissen, doch giebt er zu, dass die bezeichnung *al in balade* (l. 79) eher für die *Compl. of the Bl. Kn.* passe als für den *Temple of Glas*.

Neben diesem äusseren beweis spricht auch der innere beweis ebenso überzeugend für Lydgate als verfasser. Der ganze stil des gedichtes ist durchaus Lydgatisch; eine menge von Lydgate's charakteristischen phrasen finden sich in der *Compl.* wieder (vgl. Anmerkungen), seine „self-deprecatory vein" tritt auch hier zu tage, indem er bittet, die strafe auf ihn zu legen, wenn irgend etwas „mys-reported" sei; die allegorien und persönlichkeiten sind zum grössten teil dieselben, wie wir sie auch im *Temple of Glas* treffen, dem die *Compl.* in „tone and imagery" in vieler beziehung sehr ähnlich ist (vgl. Schick a. a. o. p. CXXVIII). Auch das metrum zeigt dieselben eigentümlichkeiten, wie wir sie von ihm an anderen werken gewohnt sind.

Kapitel VIII.

Datum des gedichtes.

Solange die *Complaint* als ein erzeugnis von Chaucer's Muse galt, war man der ansicht, dass er sie geschrieben habe „for John of Gaunt during his courtship of the Duchess Blaunche. Probably written after the Assembly of Foules" (Morley *Engl. Writers* II 202) zu dem zwecke sie „to present to his lady on occasion of some small misunderstanding incident to days of courtship" (Morley: *A short sketch of Engl. Lit.* p. 121). In der *Assembly of Foules* vermutete man früher eine anspielung auf die brautbewerbung des herzogs John of Gaunt; da nun dessen vermählung mit der herzogin Blaunche im jahre 1359 stattfand, so wäre die *Assembly of F.* und die *Compl.* vor das jahr 1359 zu setzen, was in beiden fällen aber nicht das richtige trifft. Denn die *Assembly* ist, wie ten Brink (Chaucer-Studien s. 127) nachwies, nicht vor dem jahre 1373 geschrieben, und bei der *Complaint* fiel diese frühe datierung mit der erkenntnis, dass sie von Lydgate herrühre. Doch haben wir damit für die sicherheit der datierung kein fuss breit festen bodens gewonnen. Eine bestimmte angabe über die zeit der abfassung findet sich in dem gedichte nicht, selbst anspielungen, die wenigstens im allgemeinen einen anhaltspunkt geben könnten, vermissen wir. Nur die behandlung des stoffes giebt uns einen gewissen anhaltspunkt, um eine annähernde datierung geben zu können.

Es ist ganz natürlich, dass ein dichter zu gewissen zeiten gewisse stoffe und ideen bevorzugt, von denen sich zu andern zeiten entweder gar keine spur mehr oder nur noch wenig anklänge in seinen gedichten finden. So können wir auch bei Lydgate auf grund der verschiedenartigkeit seiner stoffe in seiner dichterlaufbahn zwei perioden unterscheiden; die erste periode bis zum jahre 1412 reichend, in der er vollkommen

unter dem einfluss Chaucers steht und die mehr durch gedichte
aus dem gebiete der erotik und satire charakterisiert wird;
die zweite periode von 1412 bis zu seinem tode (nicht vor
1449)[1] reichend, in welcher seine langathmigen übersetzungen,
seine Heiligenleben und andere religiöse gedichte entstanden
(vgl. Schick a. a. o. p. XCIX ff.).

Die *Complaint of the Bl. Kn.* gehört nun, wie aus ihrem
inhalt und der ganzen behandlung des stoffes hervorgeht, der
ersten periode an, wir haben daher als weiteste grenzpunkte
die zeit von c. 1398—1412 als datum anzusetzen.

Doch können wir durch vergleichung mit anderen stücken
Lydgate's diese grenzpunkte noch näher zusammenrücken.
Nach den ausführungen von Schick darf wohl als ziemlich
feststehend erachtet werden, dass Lydgate den *Temple of Glas*
im jahre 1403 verfasst hat. Auch für die chronologie der
übrigen gedichte hat Schick viel wertvolles material beigesteuert und für die *Compl.* an zwei stellen (p. C u. CXV) darauf
hingewiesen, dass sie vor den *Temple of Gl.* zu setzen sei,
eine ansicht, der vollkommen beizuflichten ist; denn die *Compl.*
weist keineswegs die vollkommenheit oder besser gesagt aus-
bildung Lydgate's auf, welche wir im *Temple of Gl.* bemerken
können, was bei der lektüre beider werke sofort in die augen
springt. Ob nun Lydgate die *Compl.* vor dem jahre 1400 geschrieben hat, lässt sich nicht genau bestimmen, wahrscheinlicher ist, dass er sie nach dem jahre 1400 verfasst hat. Er
hätte es sich wohl nicht entgehen lassen, seines meisters
Chaucer zu gedenken, ihn etwa zu bitten „of his rude makyng
to have compassioun" oder sein gedicht „to correcte and
amende". Auch unmittelbar nach Chaucer's ableben wird er
sie nicht geschrieben haben, er hätte sonst ohne zweifel, wie
er es im *Envoy* zu der *Flour of Curtesie* gethan, den tod
seines meisters beklagt. Es bleibt also nur übrig, die *Com-*

---

[1] Nach der entdeckung von Mr. Kirk hat Lydgate noch 1449 gelebt;
während vorher sein leben nicht weiter als 1446 zu verfolgen war (vgl.
Zupitza, Angl. III, 532).

Die wertvollen dokumentarischen entdeckungen von Mr. Kirk, dem
„record-searcher" der Early English Text Society, sind auf veranlassung
von Furnivall zum abdruck gebracht worden im Appendix I von Mr. R.
Steele's ausgabe von Lydgate and Burgh's *Secrees of old Philisoffres.*
(E. E. T. S. E. S. LXVI.)

plaint zwischen die *Flour of Curtesie*, welche bald nach dem
25. Oktober 1400 geschrieben wurde, und den *Temple of Glas*
zu setzen, und ich glaube, dass er sie kurz vor dem *T. of Gl.*
geschrieben hat, da sie in „tone and imagery" diesem in vieler
beziehung ähnlich ist und nur in der ausführung sich dem
„more ambitious" *Temple of Gl.* als ein versuch auf dem gebiete der *Complaint* darstellt. Wir haben also anzunehmen,
dass die *Compl. of the Bl. Kn.* im jahre 1402/3[1] geschrieben
wurde.

Kapitel IX.
Inhalt und quellen des gedichtes.

Sorgenvoll und mit weh im herzen erwacht der dichter
an einem Maimorgen aus seinem schlummer. Um linderung
seiner schmerzen zu finden, beschliesst er in den wald zu
gehen. Einen fluss entlang schreitend, gelangt er in einen
mit moosigen steinen umwallten park, in dem die vöglein
singen und der mit prächtigen blumen und bäumen bepflanzt
ist (1—75). Hier findet er ein klares bächlein, an dessen ufer
er sich niederlässt und dessen frisches heilkräftiges wasser er
kostet, worauf er dann auch linderung seiner schmerzen fühlt
(76—120). Weitergehend kommt er in einen „herber", wo
er zwischen zwei bäumen einen mann in schwarz findet, mit
bleichem kummervollem angesicht und von fieberschauern
durchrüttelt, dessen klagen sein lebhaftes mitleid erwecken.
Um den grund dieser klage zu hören, verbirgt sich der dichter
zwischen büschen (120—148). Nach einer kurzen schilderung
des äusseren des mannes und einer invocation an *Niobe* und
Mirre wiederholt er die klage des mannes, in der die allegorie
und die aufzählung von liebhabern aus dem altertum und
mittelalter den grössten raum in anspruch nehmen. Der
klagende hebt an (v. 218), dass schon sein bleiches aussehen,
seine kummervolle miene und die thränen, die aus seinen
augen rinnen, den grund seiner betrübnis erklären. Seine
treue sei mit kälte und undank belohnt. Trouth sei durch

---

[1] Die datierung 1430 im N. E. D. (artikel: celured) halte ich für viel
zu spät. Dass er nach der *Pilgrimage du mounde* oder nach der *Legend
of St. Margaret* noch die *Compl. of the Bl. Kn.* geschrieben habe, ist mehr
als zweifelhaft.

Envy, Malebouche, Fals-report, Mysbeleve und Fals-suspecioun aus ihren rechten vertrieben und durch Falsnes ersetzt worden (218—268). Seine geliebte, an der sein herz mit treue hänge, habe ihn verbannt, und seine feinde in gnaden genommen (269—322). So sei es aber immer gewesen, dass liebe die treuen liebhaber zurücksetze, wogegen sie den falschen in der erlangung ihrer wünsche förderlich sei: Diesen satz belegt er nun durch anführung berühmter liebhaber, wie Palamides, Ercules, Phebus, Piramus, Tristan, Achilles, Antonyus, Arcite, Palamon, Adon, Mars und Ipomenes, welche trotz ihrer treuen dienste doch nur sorgen und kummer erlitten, während Jason, Aeneas, Tereus, Arcite und Demophon wegen ihrer falschheit bei ihren damen alles erreichten (323—399). So werde treue, mannheit, waffentüchtigkeit u. s. w. von liebe nicht gewürdigt, während falschheit und niedrige schmeichelei in gnaden aufgenommen würden (400—434). Bei all seiner treue habe ihn seine mitleidslose geliebte verbannt. Er beklage sich über Cupido, der in seiner blindheit ohne vernunft schiesse und die treugesinnten mehr verwunde als die falschen; das schlimmste dabei sei, dass er dann den verwundeten zu seinem feinde schicke, um dort hilfe zu suchen. So gehe es auch ihm, dass er sich an seinen feind wenden müsse, um seine wunden zu heilen (435—483). Er beklage seine geburt, denn die parzen hätten seinen tod schon bestimmt noch ehe er geboren. Er beklage sich über die göttin Nature, die seine geliebte mit allen reizen ausgestattet und ihr jedoch Daunger und Disdeyn als führer zur seite gestellt habe (484—504). Er flehe seine dame um gnade an und bitte sie in ihren diensten sterben zu dürfen. Sein leben und sein tod stehe in ihren händen. Wenn sie seinen tod beschliesse, so sei er bereit zu sterben; denn ihren befehlen gegenüber möchte er sich nicht ungehorsam zeigen. So liege er nun hier zwischen hoffnung und furcht, abwartend, was sie bestimmen möge (505—574) Nach dieser klage beginnt er zu seufzen und zu jammern, und zieht sich endlich in eine laube zurück (575—588). Der dichter verlässt nun sein versteck und beginnt die klage, wie er sie gehört hat, niederzuschreiben. Währenddem sieht er am himmel Venus emporsteigen, bei deren anblick er in die knie fällt und sie bei ihrer liebe zu Mars und Adon anfleht, sich des klagenden und aller treuen liebhaber anzunehmen, und ihnen die gnade

ihrer damen zu verschaffen (589—644). Unterdessen ist es
nacht geworden und der dichter begiebt sich nach hause. Mit
einem envoy (651—681) an eine „princes", seines herzens
königin, schliesst das gedicht.

Dies ist im wesentlichen der inhalt der *Complaint*. Was
den poetischen wert des gedichtes anbelangt, so ist derselbe
nicht sehr bedeutend. Verhältnismässig am besten gelungen
ist dem dichter der eingang, die schilderung von maimorgen
und park, obwol er auch hier nicht originell ist; auch den
schluss, die bitte an Venus, darf man als ziemlich gelungen
bezeichnen. Die eigentliche klage jedoch ist missraten. Schon
der beginn derselben ist nicht in dem stile gehalten, um in
dem leser das gefühl hervorzurufen, dass der dichter den
klagenden belauscht habe. Diese zusammenfassende strophe
würde eher angebracht sein, wenn der dichter sich dem manne
genähert und ihn gefragt hätte, was ihm fehle und warum er
klage. Der ton der klage vermag fast an keiner stelle das
mitleid des lesers zu erregen; was ihr hauptsächlich abgeht,
ist die natürlichkeit; denn der dichter vermochte es nicht,
sich in den gedankenkreis eines verschmähten liebhabers zu
versetzen. Die allegorischen figuren nehmen einen zu grossen
raum ein und sind auch, wie sie der klagende vorbringt, übel
angebracht. Absolut verdorben ist die klage durch die lange
aufzählung der liebhaber, die sich in dem munde des klagenden
sehr unnatürlich ausnimmt.

Quellen.

Die anregung zur abfassung der *Complaint* erhielt Lydgate
ohne zweifel durch Chaucer's *Book of the Duchesse*. Der maimorgen, an dem der dichter in den wald geht, die schilderung
von wald und wiese, das auffinden eines mannes, dessen klagen
der dichter belauscht, sind die züge, die Lydgate aus dem
B. D. entnommen und stellen das gerippe dar, das er durch
hinzufügen weiterer entlehnungen aus Chaucer's und Gower's
werken zu seiner *Compl. of the Bl. Kn.* ausstaffierte. Nicht
ohne bedeutenderen einfluss ist der *Rosenroman* geblieben, der
sowol zur einleitung als auch zur eigentlichen klage manchen
gedanken beigesteuert hat. Insbesondere hat ihm Lydgate die
allegorischen figuren Hope, Daunger, Malebouche, Envie, Jelousie

etc. entlehnt. Vers 36 ff. schliessen sich eng an *Rom. of the R.*
132 ff. an:

> Tho gan I walke thorough the mede
> Dounward ay in my pleiyng
> The ryver syde costeiyng
> And whan I had a while goon
> I saugh a gardyn right anoon
> Ful long and brood, and everydelle
> Enclosed was, and walled welle.

Das bächlein in v. 75 ff., das unter einem hügel seinen lauf
nimmt, hat sein vorbild in *Rom. of the R.* 114 f. Ebenso fand
Lydgate zu v. 79 ff. das sammetweiche gras, das an des bäch-
leins ufer wächst, im *R. R.* 1414 f. vorgezeichnet. Die schilderung der quelle des Narcissus wurde ohne zweifel hervorgerufen
durch *R. R.* 1616 ff. Die stelle über die heuchler v. 432 ist fast
wörtlich aus *R. R.* 2540 genommen.

Zu der schilderung des parkes diente ihm das *Parlement
of Foules* als muster, vgl. besonders v. 42 mit *Parl. of F.* v. 122:

> a parke walled with greene stoon.

Bei der aufzählung der bäume v. 64—77 schwebte ihm jedenfalls v. 172 ff. in *Parl. of F.* in der erinnerung vor.

Eine anspielung an die *Complaint to Pite* dürfen wir in
v. 670—74 erblicken, mit der einzigen änderung, dass an stelle
von Cruelté Daunger getreten ist.

Nicht ohne beeinflussung ist auch *Anelida and Arcite* geblieben. Directen bezug nimmt er in v. 379:

> of Thebes eke [loo] the fals Arcite.

Mehrere verse daraus, besonders aus der klage der Anelida
kehren fast wörtlich in der klage des mannes wieder; vgl.
speciell die anmerkungen zu den versen 208, 288, 316, 404,
408, 478.

Auch *Troilus and Cressida* ist mehrmals benutzt worden.
Die erste strophe unseres gedichtes erinnert sehr an die erste
strophe des zweiten buches in *Troilus*. Manche verse und
strophen sind weiterbildungen von im *Troil.* enthaltenen gedanken; vgl. die anm. zu vv. 183, 233, 354, 401. Eine sehr
charakteristische entlehnung findet sich in v. 488 f., die jedenfalls entstanden sind durch die erinnerung an *Troil.* III. 684:

O fatal sustren, which er any cloth
Me shapen was, my desteyne me sponne,

wobei auch noch v. 708 der *Knightes Tale*:

that shapen was my deth er that my shert

mitgewirkt haben mag. Auf die *Knightes Tale* selbst nimmt er bezug in v, 368.

V. 359 ist eine fast wörtliche wiederholung des ersten verses der *Maunciples Tale*.

Die geschichte von Phyllis und Demophon mag ihm, wie Schick a. a. o. p. CXXVII schon für den *Temple of Glas* bemerkt hat, Gower's *Confessio Amantis* geliefert haben; es scheint dies um so wahrscheinlicher, weil er in v. 380:

And Demophon ekë for his slouth

Demophon dieselbe charaktereigentümlichkeit beilegt wie Gower *Confessio* II. s. 26 es tut, wo dieser zur erläuterung des begriffes „slouth" den genius die geschichte von Phyllis and Demophon erzählen lässt. Auch den namen „philbert" (v. 68) wird er aus Gower's *Confessio* II. s. 30 genommen haben. Woher Gower diese bezeichnung hat, ist noch nicht nachgewiesen.

Holthausen in Angl. XVI s. 266 verweist auf einen commentar zu Theodulus: Phillis .... suspendit se in arborem propter absentiam Demophontis. Et quidam dicunt, quod hoc factum est in *corylo*, nam adhuc fructus illius arboris dicitur phillidis. Damit ist aber noch nicht der name „philbert" erklärt.

Ueber die geschichte von Palamides, die er aus dem *prosaroman von Tristan* entnommen haben wird, vgl. die anmerkung zu v. 329 ff.

Kapitel X.
Dart's bearbeitung der Complaint of the Bl. Kn.

Angeregt durch Dryden's[1], Pope's[2] und Sewell's[3] bemühungen, ihren zeitgenossen gedichte Chaucer's in modernem gewande darzubieten. um sie dadurch einer unverdienten vergesslichkeit zu entreissen und die „Beauties and the fine Turn

---

[1] Vgl. Schöpke, Angl. II. 314 und III. 35.
[2] Vgl. Uhlemann, Angl. VI. 107.
[3] Sewell soll nach Dart „Cupid's Proclamation" bearbeitet haben.

and genteel Sharpness of his Wit" (Dart's Preface zu seiner bearbeitung) einer grösseren allgemeinheit zugänglich zu machen, nach Dart speciell auch den damen, „that he [Chaucer] may be fashionable to keep Company with the Ladies, who otherwise are deprived of Conversing with the greatest Poet that England (or perhaps the World) euer produc'd" — angeregt dadurch hat John Dart[1]) im jahre 1718 die *Complaint of the Black Knight* modernisiert. Er sagt darüber: „I choose this Piece as a Specimen of his Love-Poetry, of which he was certainly a most excellent Master, not Second to Ovid himself as is plain from his Romaunt of the Rose, Troilus and Crescide, la belle Dame sans mercie, and this Complaint, which I think is the best design'd of any extant, either Ancient, or Modern, the Introduction (tho' long) just and beautiful; the Thoughts in the Speech natural, soft, and easy; and the Hint for Invoking Venus and the Invocation inimitable."

Ueber den schauplatz und den titel des gedichtes sagt er: „As for bringing his Complaint in a Wood, Virgil introduces himself so in his second Eclogue, and his favourite Gallus (a Person of the same Quality with ours, a knight) is brought to make his Complaint in the same Manner: And as to the Title of the black knight, he had the Authority of Homer's Memnon."

Dart's bearbeitung, die aus 566 fünftaktigen, jambischen besteht, hält sich ziemlich frei an sein original; es ist weniger eine modernisation nach dem muster von Dryden, als vielmehr eine paraphrase. Dart zeigt darin ziemliche herrschaft über das metrum, gewandtheit im ausdruck und einen leicht dahinfliessenden stil.

Als probe mögen die ersten zwanzig verse der bearbeitung dienen:

In that soft Time when Nature youthful grows
And over Hills, and Vales, profusely throws
Fressh Flow'rs of various Colours white, and red;
When balmy Gales fleet smoothly o'er the Mead:
Where Venus dances, and the Graces lead,

---

[1] John Dart, ein altertumsforscher, hat sich viel mit Chaucer beschäftigt und steuerte den grössten teil zu der biograph. einleitung in Urry's Chaucer Edition 1721 bei; vgl. darüber Lounsbury „Studies in Chaucer" I. 288.

Her shining Cistus deck with glowing Flow'rs
While smiling Springs leads on the painted Hours.
The sun ascending, shot a warmer Ray;
In larger Circles wheel'd his shining Way
Through Taurus lightsome Realms, and bore the Day.
One Morn, when in the West appear'd afar
(To chace the Night) the sober Morning-Star
From Lovers Eyes to drive the Sleep away
And call the early Vot'ries of the Day;
To glad their Souls with her returning Light
And purge the dreary Visions of the Night;
Waking I sigh'd and left my weary Bed,
To walk the Fields, and seek the Green-Wood Shade
To hear the early Birds their Mattins try
When Morning clears and hazy Vapours fly;

u. s. w.

The Complaint of the Black Knight.

1.

In May, when Flora, the fressh[e] lusty quene,
The soyle hath clad in grene, rede, and white;
And Phebus gan to shede his stremes shene
Amyd the Bole, wyth al the bemes bryght;   4
And Lucifer, to chace awey the nyght,
Ayen the morowe our orysont hath take,
To byd[de] [lovers] out of her slepe awake,

2.

And hertys heuy for to recomforte   8
From dreryhed of heuy nyghtis sorowe,
Nature bad hem ryse[n] and disporte,

---

1) fressh̄e] f. D;   2) hath] hadde P; grene, rede, and white] red grene and white T; grene whit and red S; rede quhite grene aricht Arc.S, Ch; 3) shede] shewe P;   4) Amyd] Amyddes S; the²] his Arc.S, Ch; al the bemes bryght] bemys of delyte S;   5) awey the nyght] þe night als tyte S;   6) the] f. T, P, D; hath] hadde P, S;   7) lovers] in F am rande durch eine spätere hand „louwers" hinzugefügt; f. T, W; al louers Th; awake] to wake S; 9] dreryhed] sluggerdy W; of] out of S; and Arc.S, Ch, W; heuy] f. S; any P;   10) disporte] hem disporte Th.

Ageyn the goodly, glad[e], grey[e] morowe;
And Hope also, with saint[e] John to borowe   12
Bad in dispite of Daunger and Dispeyre,
For to take the holsome lusty eyre.

3.

And with a sygh [I] gan for to abreyde
Out of my slombre, and sodenly out stert   16
As he, alas, that nygh for sorowe deyde,
My sekenes sat ay so nygh myn hert
But for to fynde socour of my smert,
Or attelest summe relesse of [my] peyn,   20
That me so sore halt in euery veyn,

4.

I rose anon, and thoght I wol[de] goon
*Into the wode, to her the briddes sing,
When that the mysty vapour was agoon,   24
And clere and feyre was the morow[e]nyng,
The dewe also *lik syluer in shynyng
Vpon the leves, as eny bavme suete,
Til firy Tytan with hys persaunt hete   28

5.

Had dried vp the lusty lycour nyw
Vpon the herbes in [the] grene mede,
And that the floures of mony dyuers hywe
Vpon *her stalkes gunne for to sprede,   32
And for to splay out her leves on brede

---

11) goodly] f. W;   12) also] f. Arc. S, Ch;   John] Johan S, Th, W;
13) Dispeyre] despeyne S;   14) to] vn to S;   to go Arc. S;   the] to T;
15) And] þoo S;   I] f. F;   for to] to Arc. S, Ch;   slombre] slombres S;   out
stert] vpstert T, P, D, Th, Arc. S, Ch;   17) nygh] night P;   18) hert]
smert P;   19) of my] f. W;   20) attelest] at leste T;   at þe leste
D, Th, S, Arc. S, Ch;   my] f. F, W;   21) so[full W;   halt] haldeþe S;
held P, Arc. S, Ch, W;   22) anon] als swiþe S;   me vp W;   I⁻] þat I Arc. S;
wolde goon] wyll anone W;   23) *Into] Vnto F, W, D;   to her] and here
P, S;   24) agoon] all gone Arc. S, Ch;   25) the[al þe S;   morowenyng]
dawing Arc. S, Ch;   26) *lik] lykyng F, lyenge lyke W;   28) persaunt]
persing S;   30) the] f. F;   euery W;   31) that] at S;   32) *her] the F;
gunne] gann D, W;   33) to] f. T;   on] in T, P, D, Th. S, Ch.

Ageyn the sun*n*e, golde-borned in hys spere,
That doun to hem cast hys bemes clere.

6.

And by a Ryuer forth I gan costey,   36
Of water clere as berel or cristal,
Til at the last I founde a lytil wey
Tovarde a pa*r*ke, enclosed with a wal
Iu compas rounde, and by a gate smal, 40
[W]ho-so that wolde, frely myght[e] goon
Into this parke, walled with grene stoon.

7.

And in I went to her the briddes songe,
Which on the braunches, bothe iu pleyn [and] vale, 44
So loude songe that al the *wode ronge,
Lyke as hyt sholde sheuer in pesis smale;
And as me thoght, that the nyghtyngale
Wyth so grete myght her voys gan out[e] wrest, 48
Ryght as her hert for love wolde brest.

8.

The soyle was pleyu, smothe, and wonder softe,
Al ouer-sprad wyth tapites that Nature
Had made her-selfe, celured eke a-lofte 52
With bowys grene, the flo[u]res for to cure,
That in her beaute they may *longe endure

---

34) golde-borned] as golde S. 35) hem] hym D; 36) forth]
f. S; forth I gan] I gan forth P; com*m* I forth Arc. S, Ch; costey] to
costey S; 39) Tovarde] Tovardes S; 41 that] f. P, W; 42) Into]
Within Arc. S., in till Ch; this] the T; with grene] with grete D;
so with S; 43) in I] I iu S; the] f. P; 44) on the] iu Arc. S, Ch; both
in] and in Arc. S, Ch; and] þe S; and] f. F, T, D, S, Arc. S, Ch; vale]
walle P; 45) songe] they songe T; were S; *wode] world F,
W, P; park S; londe Ch; 46) hyt] his T; 47) me] my P; uyghtyngale]
nyghtgale Ch; 48) her voys gan] gan hir voyce S; wrest] wraste T, D;
brest Arc. S; 49) as] as she D; brest] braste D; to brest S, Arc. S, Ch;
52) celured] syloured S, siluered Arc. S, Ch, coloryt P, D, W, couered T, Th;
a-loft] on lofft S; 53) cure] couer P; 54) That in] f. T, *weil ecke des
blattes abgerissen*; they] the T; may] might S; *longe] not longe F, W,
T, P.

Fro al assaute of Phebus feruent fere,
Which in his spere so hote shone and clere.   56

9.

The eyre atempre, and the smothe wynde
Of Zepherus, among the blosmes whyte,
So holsomme was, and so norysshing be kynde,
That smale buddes, and rounde blomes lyte,   60
In maner gan of her brethe delyte,
To yif vs hope [that] their frute shal take
Ayens autumpne, redy for to shake.

10.

I sawe ther Daphene, closed vnder rynde,   64
Grene laurer, and the holsomme pyne,
The myrre also, that wepeth euer of kynde,
The Cedres high, vpryght as a lyne,
The philbert eke, that lowe dothe enclyne   68
Her bowes grene to the erthe dovne
Vnto her knyght icalled Demophovne.

11.

Ther saw I eke [the] fressh[e] haw[e]thorne
In white motele, that so soote doth smelle,   72
Asshe, firre, and oke, with mony a yonge acorne,
And mony a tre mo then I can telle;
And me beforne I sawe a litel welle,
That had his course, as I gan beholde,   76
Vnder an hille, with quyke stremes colde.

---

55) assaute] assautes P; 56) shone and] is so and W; is schene and Arc. S, (is *f.*) Ch; shone so hote and P, S;   57) atempre] atempred P; 58) Zepherus] Phebus Arc. S, Ch, feyre Phebus S;   59 and] *f.* S; so²] *f.* Arc. S, Ch; 60) buddes] hriddes S, Arc. S; lyte] white T; 61) gan] can S; brethe] birthe S, bright P; 62) that] *nur in* S, Arc. S, Ch; their] thai Arc. S, the eyre W;   shal] shulde S;   64) ther] the T, P, D, Th, S, Arc. S, Ch; closed vnder] clothir D; rynde] lynde S; 65) Grene] þe grene S; laurer] laurell D; and] and eke Arc. S;   66) wepeth euer of] euer wepith by D; 67) Cedres] Cedre D; hye cidrice Arc. S, Ch; vpryght] as vpryght W; 68) that] whiche S; 69) Her] His Arc. S; to] vnto Arc. S, Ch; dovne] adowne S, Arc. S, Ch, Th; 70) her] his Arc. S; icalled] called T, P, D, Th, S, Arc. S, Ch; 71) the] *f.* F; 73) oke with] eke D; yonge] fressh T; 74) can] *f.* D; 75) And me beforne] þat hade his S; 76) That] And T; gan] can W, S, Arc. S, Ch.

12.

The grauel golde, the water pure as glas
The bankys rounde, the welle environyng
And softe as veluet the yonge gras,   80
That ther vpon lustely gan s[pr]yng,
The sute of trees about[e] compassyng
Her shadowe cast, closyng the wel[le] rounde,
And al *the erbes grovyng on the grounde.   84

13.

The water was so holsom, and so vertnous,
Throgh myghte of erbes grovynge [ther] beside;
*Nat lyche the welle wher as Narci[ss]ns
Islayn was thro vengeaunce of Cupide,   88
Wher so couertely he did[e] hide
The greyn of deth vpon ech[e] brynk,
That deth mot folowe, who that euere drynk.

14.

Ne lyche the pitte of the Pegace,   92
Vnder Parnaso, wher poetys *slept,
Nor lyke the welle of [pure] chastite,
Which as Dyane with her nymphes kept,
When she naked in to the water lept,   96
That slowe Acteon with his ho[u]ndes felle,
Oonly for he cam so nygh the welle.

---

78) golde] like golde Arc. S, Ch; colde D; 79) the²] þat S; 80 And] And als P; veluet] violet P; the] was the Arc. S, Ch; 81) vpon] ahowte S; lustely] so lustely S, full lustily Arc. S; gan spryng] came spryngyng T, P, D, Th; 82) sute] nowmer Arc. S, Ch; 84) *the erbes] therbes F; 85) was] f. D, S; so²] f. Arc. S, Ch; 86) erbes] þerbes S; ther] nur in S, Arc. S; 87) *Nat] That F, W; nought S; wher as] which S; Narcissus] Narcius F, W, T, D; Marcius P; 88) Islayn] Slayn W, Arc. S, Ch; thro] through the Arc. S; 89) Wher so] Quhare fore Arc. S; couertely] coniunctly Ch; hide] abyde S, Arc. S, Ch; 90) greyn] grennes W, greef S; of deth] of cruell deth Arc. S; vpon] wp P; eche] the P, Arc. S, Ch; vpon euer yche a S; 91) That] For Arc. S, Ch; mot] myght W; euere] euer hit S, Arc. S, Ch; 92) lyche] liche to Arc. S, Ch; the²] f. Arc. S, Ch, W; of the Pegace] vnder purgatorye S; 93) Vnder] Or of S; wher] where þat S, Arc. S, Ch; *slept] splept F; 94) Nor] Ne S; pure] f. F, W; 95) as] f. W; þat S; ye Th; 96) into] in T, Arc. S, Ch; 97) Acteon] Actioun D; Akoun S; Arceon Arc. S; Anceon Ch; his] her D, Th, S., Arc. S; houndes] handis D, S, W; 98) nygh] neyr P,

15.

But this welle, that I her reherse,
So holsom was, that hyt wolde aswage   100
Bollyn hertis, and the venym *perce
Of pensifhede, with al the cruel rage,
And euermore refresh[e] the visage
Of hem that were in eny werynesse   104
Of gret labour, or fallen in distresse

16.

And I that [had] throgh daunger and disdeyn
So drye a thrust, thoght I wolde assay
To tast a draght of this welle or tweyn,   108
My bitter langour yf hyt myght alay,
And on the banke anon dovne I lay,
And with myn hede *vnto the welle *I raght,
And of the water dranke I a good draght.   112

17.

Wherof me thoght I was refresshed wel
Of the brynnyng that sate so nyghe my hert,
That verely anon I gan to fele
An huge part relesed of my smert;   116
And therwith-alle anon vp I stert,
And thoght I wolde walke[n] and se more,
Forth in the parke and in the holtys hore.

18.

And thorgh a launde as I yede apace,   120
And gan about fast[e] to beholde,
I fonde anon a delytable place,
That was beset with trees yong and olde,

---

99) this] this ilke Arc. S; that] whiche S; 100) wolde] wolbe W;
101) Bollyn] Belyng Arc. S, Ch; Swollen W; *perse] perysh F, W, T, P;
103] euermore] ouyrmore T, Th; 104) were] beon S; werynesse] heuin-
esse Ch; 105) fallen] fellen P; 106) had] f. F.; 107) I] þat I Arc. S;
108 welle] f. T, P, D; 109) bitter] mattur P; 110) dovn] adoun Arc. S;
111) *vnto] into F, W, P; welle] wall P; I raght] araght F; 112) dranke
I] I dranke W, P, S; I] f. Arc. S, Ch; str. 17 und 18 fehlen in Arc. S, Ch;
114) sate] seet S; 117) therwith-alle] yer with alon P; 119) Forth]
Yet forth W; in²] f. S; 120) yede] went P; apace] in pace P; 121) *And
I F, W; gan] can S; 122) a] in a T.

Whos names her for me shal not be tolde, 124
Amyde of which stode an erber grene,
That benched was with colours nyw and clene.

19.

This erber was ful of floures *ynde,
Into the whiche as I beholde gan, 128
Betwex an hulfere and a wodebynde,
As I was war, I sawe *wher lay a man
In blake and white colour, pale and wan,
And wonder dedely also of his hiwe, 132
Of hurtes grene, and fressh[e] woundes nyw;

20.

And ouer-more destreyned with sekenesse,
Besyde *al this he was [ful] greuosly,
For upon him he had a hote accesse, 136
That day be day him shoke ful petously,
So that for *constreynt of his malady,
And hertly wo, thus lyinge al alone,
Hyt was a deth for to *here him grone. 140

21.

Wherof astonied my fote I gan with-drawe,
Gretly wondring what hit myght[e] be,
That he so lay and had[de] no *felawe
Ne that I coude no wyght with him se, 144
Wherof I had routhe and eke pite,

---

124) her for me] for me here P; her] *f.* D; me] my S;   125) Amyde]
Amiddes S; of] *f.* D; which] the which T, P, D;   126) colours] turues W;
127) floures] erbis D; *ynde] of Inde S. Arc. S, Ch; Jeude T, yende P,
gende Th; rende F, rynde W;   128) gan] can S, Arc. S, Ch;   129) Betwex]
Atuix Ch; Bytwene W; hulfere] haselle S; hoser Ch; lorere Arc. S;
130) As I was] So was I S; I²] and S; *wher] ther F;   131) white]
with D; colour] of colour P; coloured S;   132) also] was he also Arc. S,
Ch; of] *f.* W; his] *f.* D, Arc. S, Ch;   133) fresshe] fresshly S;   134) ouer-
more] enermore W, P, Arc. S, Ch;   135) *al this] as thus F, W; ful] *f.* F, W;
136) he] *f.* T, P; hote] harde S; grete Arc. S, Ch; accesse] excesse Arc. S;
138) for] *f.* P.; sore Ch; *constreynt] constreynyng F, W, T, P, D, Th, S;
malady] lady T;   139) lyinge] lyand Ch; al] *f.* P, D, S, Arc. S, Ch;
140) *here] se F, W;   141) gan] can S; with-drawe] owt drawe P;
142) what] what þat S, Arc. S;   143) hadde] hade þer S; no] ne D; *fel-
awe] felowe F, P;   144) coude] couth Ch; myght P;   145) routhe] gret
rowth P, Arc. S; eke] *f.* P.

*And gan anon, so softly as I coude,
Amonge the busshes me priuely to shronde;

22.

If that I myght in eny wise espye,   148
What was the cause of his dedely woo,
Or why that he so pitously gan crie
On hys ffortune, and on his eure also,
With al my myght I leyde an ere to,   152
Euery worde to marke what he sayed[e],
Out of his swogh among as he abreyde.

23.

But first, yf I shal make mensyoun
Of his persone, and pleynly him discrive,   156
He was in sothe, with-out excepcioun,
To speke of manhod oon the best *on lyve,
Ther may no man ayein[es] trouthe stryve;
For of hys tyme, and of his age also,   160
He proued was, ther men shuld haue ado.

24.

For oon the best ther of brede and lengthe
So wel ymade by good proporsioun,
Yf he had be in his delyuer strengthe,   164
But thoght and sekenesse wer occasioun,
That he thus lay in lamentacioun
Gruffe on the grounde, in place desolate,
Sole by him-self, aw[h]aped and amate.   168

---

146) *And] I F, W; gan] can Ch; þanne S; 146) so] as P;
147) me priuely] priuely me Th; me peyuyly T; 148) in] f. T; 150) so
pitously gan] gan so pitiously to T; gan] cau S; 151) On¹²] of S; on²]
f. Ch; his²] f. Th; eure] feuer W; 152) an] myne W, S, Ch; to] þer
to S; 153) what] quhat þat Arc. S; 154) swogh] swowne W; abreyde]
brayde W; 155) shal] shulde T, D, Th, S, Arc. S, Ch; 157) with-out]
with P; excepcioun] eny excepcioun P, W; 158) speke] take D; oon]
oon of S, D, W; *on lyve] of lyve F, P, alyue W; 159) trouth] the
treuth Arc. S; through P; 160) of²] f. P; 161) men] man T, D, a
man P; 162) oon] oon of D, W; ther] therto Th; both Arc. S, Ch;
163) ymade] made W; 166) he thus] her þer S; 167) Gruffe] Groue-
lynge W; on] and on T; in D; in place] f. T; in þat place S; al P;
168) Sole] So T; awhaped] awaked W; he wept Arc. S, Ch; amate] as
amate T, as mate P; was mate Arc. S, Ch, mate W.

25.

And for me semeth that hit ys sytting
His wordes al to put in remembraunce,
To me that herde al his compleynyng
And al the grounde of his woful chaunce,   172
Yf ther-with-al I may yow do plesaunce,
I wol to yow so as I can anone,
Lych as he seyde, reherse[n] euerychone.

26.

But who shal *helpe me now to compleyn?   176
Or who shal now my stile guy or lede?
O Nyobe! let now thi teres reyn
Into my penne, and eke helpe in this nede
Thou woful Mirre that felist my hert[e] blede   180
Of pitouse wo, and my honde eke quake,
When that I write for this mannys sake.

27.

For vnto wo acordeth compleynyng,
And delful chere vnto heuynesse,   184
To sorow also sighing and wepyng,
And pitouse morenyng vnto drerynesse,
And who that shal write[n] *of distresse,
In partye nedeth to know[e] felyngly   188
Cause and rote of al such malady.

28.

But I alas that am of wytte but dulle
And haue no knowyng of suche mater,

---

169) that] *f.* D; syttyng] fyttyng P, W;   173) ther-with-al] therwith
T, P, D; I] hit S; yow] *f.* W; yow do] do you D, S, Arc. S, Ch;   174) so]
f. P; to yow so] his wordis ry*gh*t Arc. S, Ch;   175) rehersen] reherse hem
D (thame Arc. S, Ch);   176) *Strophenüberschrift in* S: La complaynt du
Chiualier;   176) *helpe] now helpe F; now] *f.* P; to] for to S, Arc. S;
177) guy] guyde W;   178) O Nyobe] Caliope D; o eyen two Arc. S, Ch;
thi] the W; zoure Arc. S, Ch;   179) eke helpe] helpe eke T, D, Th, S, Ch;
helpe now P, Arc. S; this] *f.* T;   180) that] þowe S, Arc. S, Ch; felist]
felith D;   182) When] What P; write] write eke Arc. S, Ch;   187) who] quhoso
Arc. S; *of] to F;   188) to] for to S;   189) Cause] The cause Arc. S, Ch;
al such] suich a Arc. S, Ch;   190) but²] so T, P;   191) haue] has Ch;
knowyng] knowelage Arc. S, Ch; no knowyng have D; suche] no suche S;
the D.

For to discryve and wryte[n] at the fulle 192
The woful compleynt, which that ye shul here;
But euen-like as doth a skryuener,
That can no more what that he shal write,
But as his maister beside dothe endyte; 196

29.

Ryght so fare I, that of no sentement
Sey ryght noght as in conclusioun,
But as I herde, when I was present,
This man compleyn wyth a pytouse soun; 200
For euen-lych, wythout addissyoun,
Or disencrese, outher mor or lesse,
For to reherse anon I wol me dresse.

30.

And yf that eny now be in this place, 204
That fele in love brennyng or fervence,
Or hyndered were to his lady grace,
With false tonges, that with pestilence
Sle trwe men, that neuer did offence 208
In worde ne dede, ne in their entent,
Yf eny such be here now present,

31.

Let hym of routhe ley to audyence
With deleful chere, and sobre contenaunce, 212
To here this man be ful high sentence,

---

192) discryve] discerne S, Arc. S, Ch; wryten] wit S; 193) which]
ye whiche S; that] as T; 194) like] f. D; as] and P; 195) no] ne Ch;
what] bot Arc. S, Ch; that] f. D; 196) But] Ryght Arc. S, Ch; beside]
besyde him S, Arc. S, Ch; 197) no] f. S; 198) Sey] Ne say S; Can say
Ch; as] f. T, P, D, Th, Ch; 199) when] quhen þat Arc. S, Ch; 200) com-
pleyn] complayned W; complaint P; compleynyng Arc. S; soun] sound S;
202) Or] Off Arc. S, Ch; disencrese] difference S; disseuerance Arc. S; dis-
seueren Ch; 203) anon] f. Ch; 204) And] But S; 205) love] louyng
Arc. S, Ch; or] of Ch; 206) Or] So S; to] in to Ch; in Arc. S; vnto S;
lady] ladies W, D, Th, S, Arc. S, Ch; 207) that] and S; or Arc. S, Ch;
208) Sle] To sle Arc. S, Ch; men] men dede D; 209) ne¹] nor T, P, D,
Th, Ch; nor in Arc. S; nen S; ne²] neuer S; as Arc. S; f. Ch; 210) such]
f. P; be here now] be now here T; now he heir P; present] in present Ch;
212) deleful] wofull D; 213) ful high] ful his S; high f. W; wofull D;

His mortal wo, and his perturbaunce
Compleynyng, now lying in a traunce,
With loke up-cast, and [with ful] reuful chere,   216
Theffect of which was as ye shal here.

32. Compleynt.

The thoght oppressed with inward sighes sore,
The peynful lyve, the body langwysshing,
The woful gost, the hert[e] rent and tore,   220
The petouse chere pale in compleynyng,
The dedely face lyke asshes in shynyng,
The salt[e] teres that fro myn yen falle,
Parcel *declare grounde of my peynes alle.   224

33.

Whos hert ys grounde to blede *in heuynesse,
The thoght resseyt of woo and of compleynt,
The brest is chest of dule and drerynesse,
The body eke so feble and so feynt,   228
With hote and colde my acces ys so meynt,
That now I shyuer for defaute of hete,
And hote as glede now sodenly I suete.

34.

Now hote as fire, now colde as asshes dede,   232
Now hote for colde, *now colde for hete ageyn,
Now colde as ise, now as coles rede
For hete I bren, and thus *betwyxe tweyn

---

214) perturbaunce] grete perturbance Arc. S;   215) Compleynyng]
Compleyne Arc. S, Ch; now] now and T;   216) loke] lokes T, P, D, Th;
with ful *nur in* S, Arc. S, Ch (ful *f.* Ch);   217) Theffect] The fytte W;
as] *f.* P;   218) *in* F *mit roter tinte daneben geschrieben:* Compleynt;
sighes] thoughtis D;   220) rent] to rent S; all rent Arc. S; and] and and
W;   221) *f. in* P;   223) falle] shall W;   224) parcel] playn can Ch;
*declare] declared F; grounde] the grounde D, S, Ch;   225) peynes] peyne
Ch;   225) grounde] grownded D; bound Arc. S; *in] on F, W;   226) res-
seyt] resort S; of²] *f.* S, Arc. S, Ch;   227) is] *f.* D; hote] hete S; ys] ben
Arc. S; so meynt] ymeynte T;   230) shyuer] chele S; chill Arc. S, Ch;
232) hote as] as a S; now²] and Arc. S, Ch;   233) for¹·²] fro T, P, D;
from Arc. S, Ch; for¹] now S; for²] fro S; *now colde] *f.* F, W; and cold
Arc. S, Ch; hete] hote P, S, Arc. S, Ch;   234) colde as ise] as yse colde D;
now²] and now; now hote Arc. S, Ch; coles rede] firy glede D; *betwyxe]
betwext F; betuixen Arc. S; betwene D, W;

I possed am, and al forcast in peyn, 236
So that my *hete pleynly as I fele
Of greuouse colde ys cause euery dele.

35.

This ys the colde of ynwarde high dysdeyn,
Colde of dyspite, and colde of cruel hate; 240
This is the colde that euere doth [his] besy peyn,
Ayen[e]s trouthe to fighte[n] and debate;
This ys the colde that wolde the fire abate
Of trwe menyng, alas, the harde while, 244
This ys the colde that will me begile,

36.

For euere the better that in trouthe I ment,
With al my myght feythfully to serue,
With hert and al to be diligent, 248
The lesse thanke, alas, I can deserue.
Thus for my trouthe Daunger doth me sterue;
For oon that shuld my deth of mercie let,
Hath made Dispite now his suerde to whet 252

37.

Ayen[e]s me, and his arowes to file,
To take vengeaunce of wilful cruelte
And tonges fals throgh her sleghtly wile
Han gonne a werre that wol not stynted be 256
And fals Envye of wrathe, and Enemyte

---

236) possed] passed W; am] *f.* T; al] *f.* P, D; 237) *hete Th] colde *die übrigen hs. u. dr.*; as I fele] euery dele S; 238) greuouse] greuance Arc. S, Ch; colde] hert D; euery dele] of myn vnseele S; 239) dysdeyn] distresse Arc. S, Ch; 241) euere] *f.* Arc. S, Ch; his] *f.* F, W; besy] *f.* S; peyne] hate T; besy peyne] besynesse Arc. S, Ch; 242) and] and to Arc. S, Ch; and make W; 243) *This] Thus F; wolde] *f.* Th; 245) will] wolde T, S, Arc. S, Ch; 246) euere] *f.* S; better] het Arc. S; that in trouthe] þat I in trouthe S; the trouth I W; þat I treuth Arc. S, Ch; 248) to] for to Arc. S; be diligent] diligence P; 249) can] gan W; 250) Thus] þat S; me sterue] desterue Ch; 252) Hath] Hade P; now] newe T, P, Th; 253) arowes] arow T; to] *f.* Arc. S, Ch; 254) of] and P; 255) sleghtly] sleghty S, Arc. S, W; sely P; wile] whyle W; 256) Han] Hath W; And hath D; Thanne P; gonne] begon D, W; 257) And] Of S, Arc. S, Ch, W; of] *f.* Th;

Haue conspired ayens al ryght and lawe,
Of her malis, that Trouthe shal be slawe.

38.

And Male-bouche gan first the tale telle,   260
To sclaundre Trouthe of indignacioun,
And Fals-report so loude ronge the belle,
That Mys-beleve and Fals-suspecioun
Haue Trouthe brought to hys dannacioun,   264
So that alas wrongfully he dyeth,
And Falsnes now his place occupieth,

39.

And entred ys into Trouthes londe,
And hath therof the ful possessyoun.   268
O ryghtful God! that first the trouthe fonde,
How may thou suffre such oppressyoun,
That Falshed shuld have jurysdixioun
In Trouthes ryght, to sle him gilt[e]les?   272
In his fraunchise he may not lyve in pes.

40.

Falsly accused, and of his foon for-iuged,
Without *ansuer, while he was absent,
He damned was, and may not ben excused: 276
For Cruelte satte in jugement
Of hastynesse with-out avisement,
And bad Disdeyn do execute anon
His jugement in presence of his fon.   280

---

258) Haue] Hath Arc. S; al] *f.* S;   259) Trouthe] throw I Arc. S, Ch;
right S; slawe] drawe P;   260) gan] can S;   261) Trouthe of] throw on
P;   263) suspecioun] euspicioun P;   264) Haue] Hath D; brought] ybroght
P, Arc. S, Ch; dannacion] dampcyoun W;   266) now] *f.* W; Falsnes now
his place] his place now falsnes Arc. S, Ch;   267) Trouthes] trouthe his P;
268) hath] hat T; the] *f.* Arc. S, Ch; ful] fully Ch;   269) the] *f.* D, S;
271) shuld] *f.* W;   272) to] and S;   273) In] And in S; he] *f.* S; lyve]
lyen T;   274) accused] for-juged S; of] by S; for-iuged] accused S;
275) Without] Withouten P, Arc. S, Ch; *ansuer] vnsuer F; while] whiles
S;   278) with-out] withouten P;   279) do] don T; to D; be Ch;

41.

Atturney non ne may admytted ben
To excuse Trouthe, ne a worde to speke;
To Feyth or Othe the juge list not sen,
Ther ys no geyn but he wil be wreke.   284
O Lorde of Trouthe! to the I calle and clepe,
How may thou se thus in thy presence,
With-out[e] mercy mordred Innocence

42.

Now God! that art of Trouthe souereyn,   288
And seest how I lye for trouthe bounde,
So sore knytte in loves firy cheyn,
Euen at the deth thro-girt with mony a wounde,
That lykly ar neuer for to sounde,   292
And for my trouthe am damned to the dethe,
And noght abide but drawe alonge the brethe,

43.

Consider and se in thyn eternal sight,
How that myn hert professed whilom was,   296
For to be trwe with al my ful[le] myght
Oonly to oon the which[e] now, alas!
Of volunte, withoute more trespas,
Myn accusurs hath taken vnto grace,   300
And cherissheth hem my deth for to purchace.

---

281) non ne may] ne *f.* P, S; may noon D, Th, Arc. S, Ch; may not
T; admytted] accepted S;   282) ne] *f.* W; ne a worde] now inward Arc.
S, Th; to] *f,* S;   283) or] nor Arc. S, Ch; Oth] soth Arc. S; not] to P, W;
284) ys no geyn] gayneþe nought S; wil] wolde S;   285) clepe] cleke
Arc. S; speke D;   286) thus] this W;   287) mordred] murder Arc. S; to
mordir D;   289) bounde] ybound Arc. S, Ch;   290) *vers f. in* P; So] *f.* S,
Arc. S, Ch; knytte] I knytte W;   291) thro-girt] throuthe gird P; ouergirt
Arc. S, Ch; hurt S; a] *f.* Arc. S, Ch;   292) That] Whiche S; ar] am W;
beon S, Arc. S, Ch; for] *f.* S; sounde] be sounde D, S;   294) abide] to
habyde Arc. S, Ch; but] and S; alonge] longer Arc. S, Ch; the] thy Arc. S,
Ch; my S;   295) sight] right T, P, D, Th, Arc. S, Ch; light S;   296) professed whilom] professit sum tyme Arc. S, Ch; some time professed S;
298) the whiche] whiche þat S;   299) more] eny T, P, D, Th, S, Arc. S, Ch;
301) cherissheth] cherysshed W; hem] hym W; for] *f.* D, Arc. S, Ch.

44.

What meneth this? what ys this wonder vre
Of purveaunce, yf I shal hit calle,
Of God of love, that fals hem so assure,   304
And trew, alas! dovn of the whele be falle?
And yet in sothe this is the worst of alle,
That Falshed wrongfully of Trouth hath the name,
And Trouthe ayenwarde of Falshed bereth the blame. 308

45.

This blynde chaunce, this stormy aventure
In love hath most his experience;
For who that doth with trouth[e] most his cure,
Shal for his mede fynde most offence,   312
That serueth love with al his diligence,
For who can feyne vnder loulyhede,
Ne fayleth not to fynde grace and spede.

46.

For I loued oon ful longe sythe agoon   316
With al my hert, body and ful[le] myght,
And to be ded my hert[e] can not goon
From his hest, but hold that he hath hight;
Thogh I be banysshed out of her syght,   320
And by her mouthe damned that I shal deye,
Vnto my behest yet I wil euer obeye.

47.

For euere sithe that the worlde began,
Who so lyste loke and in storie rede,   324

---

302) What] That S; meneth] movith D; this²] þe D;   303) Of] Or
S; yf] if þat Arc. S;   304) Of¹] On S; O Arc. S, Ch; hem] hym W; hem
so] so hem S; hem doth D; thai so Ch;   305) dovn] adowne W; the] thy
Arc. S, Ch;   307) Falshed wrongfully] wrongfully falshed Arc. S, Ch;
wrongfully] wrongwisly T; wronge S; hath] herith D, S;   308) Tronthe]
truwe S; of] as W; of Falshed] f. T, P, D; bereth] hath D, S; the] all
the P, D;   310) most his] this most W;   311) who] he S;   314) who]
quhoso Arc. S, Ch;   315) Ne] He S; fayleth] falleth Ch;   316) ful] so S;
sythe agoon] sithen gone Arc. S, Ch;   v. 319 u. 320 in S umgestellt.
319) his] hir S; my Arc. S, Ch; hest] behest Arc. S, Ch; he hath] I haue
S, Arc. S, Ch;   320) banysshed] hanned S;   321) that I shal] for to S;
322) Vnto] To S; I wil euer obeye] euer obey will I W; woll I euer
obey D, S; euer] f. Arc. S, Ch;   323) worlde] wordle D;   324) Who-so]
Quhoso þat Arc. S, Ch; loke] to loke W;

He shal ay fynde that the trwe man
Was put abake, wher-as the falshede
I furthered was; for Love taketh non hede
To sle the trwe, and hath of hem no charge,　　328
Wher-as the fals goth frely at her large.

48.

I take recorde of Palamides,
The trwe man, the noble worthy knyght,
That euer loved, and of hys peyne no relese,　　332
Not-withstondyng his manhode and his myght,
Loue vnto him did ful grete vnright,
For ay the bette he did in cheualrye,
The more he was hindred by Envye;　　336

49.

And ay the bette he dyd in enery place,
Throgh his knyghthode, and [his] besy peyn,
The ferther was he fro his ladys grace,
For to her mercie myght he neuer ateyn,　　340
And to his deth he coude hyt not refreyn
For no daunger, but ay *obey and serue,
As he best coude pleynly til he sterue.

50.

What was the fyne also of Ercules,　　344
For al his conquest and his worthynesse,
That was of strengthe alone pereles?
For lyke as bokes of him list expresse,
He set[te] *pilers thro his high provesse,　　348

---

326) the] f. D, S;　327) I-furthered] Furthered W, Arc. S; non] now
Ch;　328) the] f. P; hem] him S, W;　329) goth] goon S: her] his P,
Arc. S, Ch;　330) of] of him Arc. S; Palamides] Palymedes D; Palamadees
S;　331) the²] þat D; the noble worthy] and the nobyl P; peyne] peynes
P; of his peyne no relese] neuer hade relees S;　334) Love] None W;
vnto him did] ded to hym P;　335) bette] better T, P, D, Th, S, Ch, W;
338) his¹] his hye W; his²] f. F, W, Th;　339) ferther] ferrer P, Arc. S;
was he] he was D; ladys] lady T, P, S;　340) mercie] grace S; he] f. P;
341) hyt] f. S; not refreyn] neuyr attayne T;　342) no] to W; *obey]
wey F;　345) his²] f. W;　347) of him list] liste of him T, S, W; can of
him Arc. S, Ch;　348) *pilers] periles F; peyrles P; his] f. T, P; high]
f. D;

Away at Cades, for to signifie,
That no man myght him passe in cheualrie.

51.

The whiche pilers ben ferre by-yonde Ynde
Be-set of golde, for a remembraunce; 352
And for al that was he sete behynde
With hem that Loue list febly avaunce;
For [he] him set last vpon a daunce,
Ayen[e]s whom helpe may no strife, 356
For al his trouth [ȝit] he lost his lyfe.

52.

Phebus also for *al his persaunt lyght,
When that he went her in erthe lowe,
Vnto the hert with [fresshe] Venus sight 360
Ywounded was, thro Cupides bowe,
And yet his lady list him not to knowe,
Thogh for her love his hert[e] did[e] blede,
She let him go, and toke of him no hede. 364

53.

What shal I say of yonge Piramus?
Of trwe Tristram for al his high renovne?
Of Achilles or of *Antonyus?
Of Arcite or of him Palamovne? 368
What was the ende of her passioun?
But after sorowe dethe and then her graue.
Lo her the guerdon that [thes] louers haue!

---

349) Away] Alway P, W; So fer S; Cades] Gades Th, W, Arc. S, Ch;
Goddes P;   351) hen] f. P, Th; pilers] pyles Th;   352) Be-set] Ben sette
S; Ysett Arc. S, Ch; Sette D;   353) that] þat ȝit Arc. S, Ch; sete] put D;
354) avaunce] tavaunce S; to avaunce P, W;   355) he *nur in* S; laste] at
þe laste S; a] the D; daunce] chance P;   356) whom] quhois Arc. S, Ch;
357) ȝit *nur in* Arc. S, Ch; he] for loue he S;   358) for] wyth Ch; *al]
as F;   359) When that] Whanne S; he] she P; went] dwelt S;   360) the]
his S; hert] erthe W; fresshe Arc. S] goddes S; f. F, W, T, P, D, Th, Ch;
Venus] Phebus T;   361) Ywounded] he woundid D, S; thro] with Arc. S,
Ch; bowe] owne bowe Arc. S, Ch;   362) yet] f. S; his] this T; him not]
not hym D, S, Arc. S, Ch;   363) her] his S; f. P; for her love] he for hir
Arc. S; blede] offt blede S;   364) let] bade S;   365) Piramus] Priamus
D, S, W;   366) trwe] Troy D; high] f. S; grete D;   367) *Antonyus]
Antonyas F;   368) or] f. W; eke or Arc. S;   371) her] here is P; thes]
f. F, W;

54.

But false Iasoun with his doublenesse,   372
That was vntrwe at Colkos to Mede,
And Tereus, rote of vnkyndenesse,
And with these two eke the fals Ene.
Lo thus the fals, ay in oon degre,   376
Had in love her lust and al her wille,
And save falshed ther was non other skille.

55.

Of Thebes eke [loo] the fals Arcite,
And Demophon eke for his slouthe,   380
They had her lust and al that myght delyte,
For al her falshede and [hir] grete vntrouthe.
Thus euer Love, alas, and that is routhe,
His false legys furthereth what he may,   384
And sleeth the trwe vngoo[d]ly day be day.

56.

For trwe Adon was slayn with the bore
Amyde the forest in the grene shade,
For Venus love he felt al the sore.   388
But Vulcanus with her no mercy made,
The foule cherle *had many nyghtis glade,
Wher Mars her [worthy] knyght, her [trewe] man,
To fynde mercy comfort noon he can.   392

57.

Also the yonge fressh Ipomones,
So lusty fre as of his corage,

---

373) at Colkos] at Kokes Ch; to Kokes Arc. S; and Colkes P; and
al so S; to Mede] Ymodee S; Terens] Terens W; Theseus T, P, Th, S,
Arc. S; thecins Ch; the Thesus D; rote] the rute Arc. S;   375) these] the
thes T; Ene] gne P;   379) loo] *nur in* S;   380) his] his foule S;   381) lust]
wille S;   382) hir] *nur in* S, Arc. S;   383) euer] *f.* S; alas and that] in
that allace Arc. S; allace in that Ch; routhe] gret routhe S;   386) Adon]
Abdoun D;   387) shade] shadowe W;   389) with her no mercy] no mercy
with him S;   390) *had] and F, W;   391) her¹] the Arc. S; worthy] *nur
in* Arc. S; her²] and her T, P, D, Th, S, Arc. S, Ch; trewe] *nur in* Arc. S;
owen S;   392) comfort] nor comfort Arc. S, Ch;   393) Ipomenes] Ypomedes
Th;   394) So] A Arc. S, Ch; fre] and fre D; as] was S; and W; *f.* P;
his] her P, S, Arc. S;

That for to serue with al his hert [he] ches
*Athalant, so feire of her visage;   396
But Love, alas, quyte him so his wage
With cruel daunger pleynly at the last,
That with the dethe guerdonlesse he past.

58.

Lo her the fyne of lovers seruise!   400
Lo how that Love can his seruantis quyte!
Lo how he can his feythful men dispise,
To sle the trwe men and fals[e] to respite!
Lo how he doth the suerde of sorowe byte   404
In hertis suche as *most his lust obey,
To save the fals and do the trwe dey!

59.

For feyth or othe, worde ne assuraunce
Trwe menyng, awayte, or besynesse,   408
Stil[le] port ne feythful attendaunce,
Manhode ne myght in armes worthinesse,
Pursute of wurship, nor [no] high provesse,
In straunge londe rydinge ne trauayle,   412
Ful lyte or noght in love dothe avayle.

60.

Peril of dethe, nother in se ne londe
Hungre ne thrust, sorowe ne sekenesse,
Ne grete emprises for to take on honde,   416

---

395) he] *f.* F;   396) *Athalant] Athalans *in sämtl. hs. u. dr.*; Atlans
D; her] his S;   397) quyte him so] so quit hym T;   399) guerdonlesse]
grewusly P;   400) lovers] loues T, P, D, Th, S, Arc. S, Ch; seruise] hye
servyce S;   401) that] *f.* W; that love can] he can S, Arc. S, Ch; seruantis]
seruand Ch; quyte] hyre qwyte S;   402) how] *f.* P; men] man T;
403) men] man D, S, W; *f.* Arc. S, Ch; fals] þe fals D;   404) the] wíth
the P; byte] smyte P; 405) suche] of suche S; *most] must F, W; dope
S; his] *f.* P; lust] lustes S, Ch; love D;   406) the¹] *f.* P; dey] to dey
W;   407) nor] ne P, S, Arc. S, Ch; ne] nor Arc. S, Ch;   408) or] nor Arc.
S, Ch;   411) no] *nur in* S, Arc. S, Ch; nor] ne S;   412) londe] landis Arc.
S; ne] nor Arc. S, Ch;   414) of] nor Arc. S, Ch; nother] nor T, P, D, Th;
f. Arc. S, Ch; in] on Arc. S; ne] ne in T, D; nor on Arc. S; nor a Ch;
nor W;   415 *u.* 416 *fehlen in* P;   415) ne¹] nor Arc. S, Ch; ne²] no
Arc. S; nor Ch; 416) Ne] No D; emprises] emprise Arc. S, Ch;

Shedyng of blode, ne manful hardynesse,
Nor ofte woundynge at sawtes by distresse,
Nor *iupartyng of lyfe, nor dethe also,
Al ys for noghte, Love taketh non hede therto.   420

61.

But lesynges with her fals[e] flaterye,
Thro her falshed and with her doublenesse,
With tales new, and mony feyned lye,
By false-semlaunce, and contrefet humblesse,   424
Vnder colour depeynt with stidfastnesse,
With fraude cured vnder a pitouse face,
Accept ben now rathest vnto grace.

62.

And can hem-self now best magnifie   428
With feyned port and presumpsioun
They haunce her cause with fals surquedrie,
Under menyng of double entencioun,
To thenken on in her opynyoun   432
And sey another, to set hym-selfe alofte,
And hynder tr[o]uthe, as hit ys seyn ful ofte

63.

The whiche thing I bye now al to dere,
Thanked be Venus and the god Cupide!   436
As hit is seen by myn oppressed chere,
And by his arowes that stiken in my syde,
That safe the deth I no thing abide
Fro day to day, alas, the harde while,   440
When euere hys dart that hym list to fyle,

---

417) ne] nor Arc. S; no Ch;   418) Nor] Not D; Ne Th;   419) *iu-partyng] jupardy D; *die übrigen hs. u. dr.* in partyng; of] in Arc. S, Ch; nor] nor of T; or of P; and W;   421) lesynges] losingeris Ch; false] *f.* T, P, D, Th, Arc. S, Ch;   422) her²] *f.* S;   423) mony] many a P, D; 426) pitouse] double Arc. S;   427) Accept] Accepted S; Excep Ch; be now] nowe beon S; rathest] rather P; vnto] in to S;   428) cau] gan Ch; now] *f.* P, S, Arc. S, Ch; best] *f.* W;   429) and] and false Arc. S; 430) haunce] haunt P, Th; change W, S, Arc. S, Ch; with] in Arc. S, Ch; 431) Vnder] Vnder þe S;   433) another] they ought Arc. S, Ch;   435) now al] al nowe S;   436) the] hir Ch;   439) That safe] Saue only W; the] *f.* T, P, D, Th, Ch; abide] ellis abyde S;   441) that] *f.* D; hym] *f.* P;

64.

My woful hert for to ryve atwo,
For faute of mercye, and lake of pite
Of her that causeth al my peyn and woo,   444
And list not ones of grace for to see
Vnto my trouthe throgh her cruelte.
And most of al [ʒit] I me compleyn
That she hath joy to laughen at my peyn,   448

65.

And wilfully hath my dethe [y]-sworne,
Al gilt[e]les and wote no cause why,
Safe for the trouthe that I have had aforne
To her allone to serue feythfully.   452
O God of Love! vnto the I crie,
And to thy blende double deyte
Of this grete wrong I compleyn[e] me,

66.

And *to thy stormy wilful variaunce,   456
I-meynt with chaunge and gret vnstabl[en]esse,
Now vp, now down, so rennyng is thy chaunce,
That the to trust may be no. sikernesse;
I wite hit nothinge but thi doublenesse,   460
And who that is an archer, and ys blynde,
Marketh nothing, but sheteth by wenynge.

67.

And for that he hath no discrecioun,
With-oute avise he let his arowe goo,   464
For lak of syght and also of resoun,

---

442) for] *f.* S; atwo] al atwo S;   443) faute] defaute D;   445) of] of hir S; my D;   446) throgh] trwe P; for Arc. S, Ch;   447) ʒit] þat S; *f.* F, W, T, P, D, Th;   449) y-sworne Arc. S; sworne *die übrigen hs. u. dr.* 451) for] *f.* S; have] *f.* Th; had] *f.* W;   452) feythfully] most feythfully Arc. S, Ch; hir feythfully S;   453) of Love] aboue T, P, D, S, Arc. S, Ch; vnto] to T, S, W; I crie] I calle and crye S;   454) blende double] double blynde S;   455) I] thus I S; þat I now Arc. S;   456) *to] vnto F, T, P, Th; thy] the S;   457) I-meynt] Mengit Ch; vnstablenesse] doublenesse S;   458) is] in Arc. S, Ch;   459) no] ne D; sikernesse] sikenesse Ch; 460) I] aud P; hit] *f.* T, P, D;   462) by wenynge] by wende Th; as he wend Arc. S, Ch;   464) he] *f.* P; she Th; let] letith D, Arc. S, Ch; holdeþe S; arowe goo] bowe gode S.

In his shetyng hit happeth oft[e] soo,
To hurt his frende rathir then his foo;
So doth this god with his sharpe flon,   468
The trwe sleeth and leteth the fals[e] goon.

68.

And of his wou*n*dyng this is the worst of alle,
When he hurteth he dothe so cruel wreche,
And maketh the seke for to crie and calle   472
Wnto his foo for to ben his leche,
And *hard hit ys for a man to seche,
Vpon the poynt of dethe [in] iupardie,
Vnto his foo to fynde remedye.   476

69.

Thus fareth hit now euen[ly] by me,
That to my foo that yaf my hert a wounde,
Mot axe grace, mercie, and pite,
And namely ther wher noon may be founde;   480
For now my sore my leche wol confounde
And god of kynde so hath set myn vre,
My lyves foo to haue my wounde in cure.

70.

Alas the while now that I was borne!   484
Or that I euer saugh the bright[e] sonne!
For now I se that ful longe aforne,
Er I was borne, my destanye was sponne
By *Parc*as sustren, to sle me if they conne,   488
For they my dethe shopen or my shert,
Oonly for trouthe I may hit not astert.

---

466) shetyng] settyng P; 469) trwe] trwe man P, S; 470) is] *f.* Th;
471) When] Wham P, Whome þat S; he²| *f.* T, D, Th, S; so] to so T, Th;
dothe so] and so D; 472) And] He P; 474) *hard] herd F; hert P;
475) of dethe in] of a S; in] *f.* F; iupardie] jupard P; 476) to] for to
Arc. S, Ch; 477) hit] *f.* Ch; enenly] Arc. S, Ch, *die übrigen hs. u. dr.* eueu;
479) axe] are Ch; grace mercie] mercy grace Arc. S, Ch; axe grace] me
graunt S; 480) wher] *f.* B, W; noon may] may noon S; 482) so] he S;
hath] hat T; 483) my] *f.* P; wounde] wo Arc. S, Ch; 485) euer saugh]
sawe euer S, Arc. S, Ch; 486) ful] *f.* P; 487) Er] *f.* Ch; 488) By] *f.* S;
sustren] suffren S; 489) shopen] haue shapen Arc. S

71.

The myghty goddesse also of nature,
That vnder God hath the gou*er*naunce   492
Of worldly thinges com*m*ytted to her cure,
Disposed hath thro her wyse purveaunce,
To yive my lady so moche suffisaunce
Of al vertues, and therwith-al purvyde   496
To mordre Trouthe, hath taken Daunger to guyde.

72.

For bounte, beaute, shappe, and semelyhed,
Prudence, wite, passyngly fairenesse,
Benigne port, glad chere with loulyhed,   500
Of womanhed ryght plentevous largesse,
Nature in her fully did empresse,
Whan she her wroght, and altherlast Dysdeyne,
To hinder Trouthe, she made her chambreleyne.   504

73.

When Mystrust also, and Fals-suspeciou*n*,
With Mys-beleve she made for to be
Chefe of counseyle to this conclusiou*n*,
For to exile Routhe and eke Pite,   508
Out of her court to make Mercie fle,
So that Dispite now haldeth forth her reyn,
Thro hasty beleve of tales that men feyn.

74.

And thus I am for my trouthe, alas!   512
Mordred and slayn with wordis sharp and kene,
Gilt[e]les, God wote, of al trespas,

---

492) hath] haue S;   493) worldly] wordely T, wordly D; to] to
do S; cure] *f.* D;   494) Hath] Han T, P; haue D, Th, S; wyse] *f.* B, W, S;
purveaunce] *f.* T; 496) purvyde] provide S, Arc. S; 497) hath] haue T, S;
taken] *f.* D, S; guyde] hir guyde S; 498) For] Yf for W;   499) wite]
and witt Ch, and witt and Arc. S; with T, D, S;   501) largesse] largenes
T, P, Th; plentevous] plentous Ch; plenteous *and* W;   502) in her
fully did] did in her fully T, P, D, Th, Arc. S; did ful in hir Ch; did
fully in hir p*er*sone S; 505) When Mystrust] Quhau to myschef Ch; also
and] and als T, P, D; also] *f.* Arc. S, Ch; 507) this] his Th; 508) Routhe]
trouthe W, Th, Arc,. S, Ch; Pite] pietee Arc. S;   509) Oute] And oute S;
But W; to] *f.* S; make] *f.* D; 510) now haldeth] holdeþe now S; now]
f. Arc. S, Ch; her] his Arc. S, Ch; the T, P, D; 514) al] al manere S, Arc. S.

And lye and blede vpon this colde grene.
Now mercie, suete! mercye, my lyves quene! 516
And to youre grace of mercie yet I prey,
In your seruise that your man may dey.

75.

But and so be that I shall deye *algate,
And that I shal non other mercye haue, 520
Yet of my dethe let this be the date
That by youre wille I was broght to my graue,
Er hastely yf that ye list me saue
My sharpe wou*n*des that ake so and blede, 524
Of mercie charme, and also of womanhede.

76.

For other charme pleynly ys ther noon,
But only mercie, to helpe[n] in this case;
For thogh my wounde blede euere in oon, 528
My lyve, my deth *stondeth in your grace,
And thogh my gilt be nothing, alace!
I axe mercie in al my best entent,
Redy to dye yf that ye assent. 532

77.

For ther ayens shall I neu*er* strive
In worde ne werke, pleynly I ne may,
For leuer I haue then to be alyve
To dye sothely, and hit be her to pay; 536
Ye, thogh hit be this ech[e] same day,

---

516) suete] swet now P; 517) of] *f.* S; 518) that] þat I S;
519) and] if T, P, D, Th, S, Arc. S, Ch; so] hit so S; *algate] alagate F;
520) non other] neuer oþer S; no noyer P; 521) Yet] And S, Arc. S, Ch;
522) wille] *f.* T; 523) yf that] *f.* D; ye] you S, Arc. S, Ch; saue] to
saue D; 524) ake so and] eke also S; ake also and Arc. S, Ch; so] so
sore P; 525) charme] charyte W; also] als Arc. S, Ch; eke S; of] *f.* P;
526) charme] maner W; medecyne S; 527) mercie] *f.* T; to helpen] *f.*
Arc. S, Ch; lady S; case] wofull case Arc. S; 528) wounde] woundes
Arc. S, Th; euer] ouer P; 529) *stondeth] stont F, B, D, Arc. S, Ch; in]
all in Arc. S, Ch; 530) thogh] thoght Ch; 532) Redy] And redy P, S,
Arc. S, Ch; ye] ye will S; 533) shall] ne shal S; 534) ne] no Ch; nor
on Arc. S; ner in P; I ne] yif I P; 535) haue] hade S; alyve] on
lyve S; 536) To] *f.* S; hit] if P; her to] to her W, Th; yow to S.
Arc. S; 537) Ye) ȝa Arc. S, Ch; eche] *f.* Th; ilke Arc. S, Ch.

Or when that euer her lust[e] to deuyse,
Sufficeth me to dye in your seruise.

78.

And God, that knowest the thoght of eu*ery* wyght 540
Ryght *as hit is, in euery thing thou maist se,
Yet er I dye, with al my ful[le] myght,
Louly I prey to graunte[n] vnto me
That ye, goodly, feir[e], fressh, and fre 544
Which sle me oonly for defaut of routhe
Er then I die, [ye] may know my trouthe.

79.

For that in sothe suffic[et]he [vnto] me,
And she hit knowe in eu*ery* circu*m*staunce, 548
And after I am wel[a]payed that she
Yf that her list of deth to do vengeaunce
Vnto me, that am vnder her legeaunce,
Hit sitte me not her doom to dysobey, 552
But at her lust wilfully to dey.

80.

Wyth-out[e] gruching or rebelliou*n*,
In wil or worde, holy I assent,
Or eny maner contradixiou*n*, 556
Fully to be at her com*m*aundement,
And yf I dye in my testament
My hert I send, and my spirit also,
What so-euer she list with hem to do. 560

---

538) Or when] Lo whe*þ*er S; her] he P; ʒow Arc. S; to] for to S;
539) Sufficeth] Hit suffise*þ*e S; your] here D, Ch; 541) *as] at F; in
euery] al S; 543) prey] preye yow Arc. S; 544) ye] *þ*e D, S; 545) sle]
sleeth D, S, Arc. S, Ch; sle me oonly] onely sle me Th; 546) then] that
T, S, W, Th; ye] *nur in* Th, S, Arc. S, Ch; my] by my Arc. S, Ch; 547) in
sothe] truly S; vnto] *nur in* S, Arc. S, Ch; 548) And] If Arc. S, Ch; wel-
apayed] welpayed F, B, T, P, D, Th; 550) Yf] yit P; vengeaunce] greuance Arc. S, Ch; 551) Vnto] To S, Arc. S, Ch; legeaunce] allegeaunce S;
552) Hit sitte me not] ʒit shall I nat Arc. S, Ch; sitte] site*þ*e S; me not]
not me S; to] *f.* P, Arc. S, Ch; 553) at] as D, S, al Th; But at] Quhereso Arc. S, Ch; wilfully to dey] to do my lyve or deye Arc. S, Ch;
555) holy] holely P, B, W; 559) maner] maner of P, S, Arc. S, Ch;
559) my²] *f.* Ch; 560) so-euer] someuer B, W; so] *f.* P, Arc. S, Ch; euer]
f. S; she] hem S; with hem] with hit S; to] for to P, S, Arc. S, Ch.

81.

And alderlast to her womanhede,
And to her mercy me I recommaunde,
That lye now here *betwexe hope and drede,
Abyding pleynly what she list commaunde;   564
For vtterly — this nys no demaunde —
Welcome to me while me lasteth brethe,
Ryght at her cho[i]se, wher hit be lyf or dethe.

82.

In this mater more what myght I seyn,   568
Sithe in her honde and in her wille ys alle,
Bothe lyf and dethe, my joy, and al my peyn,
And fynally my hest[e] holde I shall
Til *my spirit, be destanye fa[ta]l,   572
When that her list fro my body *wende,
Haue her my trouthe and thus I make an *ende.

83.

And with that worde he gan sike as sore,
Lyke as his hert ryve wolde atweyne,   576
And holde his pese and spake a worde no more
But for to se his woo and mortal peyn,
The teres gan fro myn eyen reyn
Ful piteusly for werry inwarde routhe,   580
That I hym sawe so languysshing for his trouthe

---

561) alderlast] euermore S; to] vnto S, Arc. S;   562) mercy] f. P;
me] f. T;   me I] I me P, S, Arc. S, Ch;   563) *betwexe] betwext F, T, P;
bytwene S, W;   564) she] hir S;   nys] ne is T;   is D, W;   566) while]
whilest S;   quhile þat P, Arc. S, Ch;   me²] f. T;   she S;   my breth P;
567) wher] whedir T, D;   whether P, Arc. S, Ch, W;   f. S;   hit be] be
hit S;   568) more what myght I seyn] what myght I more seye S;
570) deth my] f. D;   571) heste] herte W;   572) *my] be my F, B, W;
be] be by D;   573) When] What P;   her] it Arc. S;   *wende] wynde
F, B;   574) *ende] ynde F, B;   575) in F, B, W als strophenüberschrift
Nota perseueranciam amantis;   575) gan] kan Ch;   sike] to sike Arc. S;
576) ryve wolde] wold ryve B, W, Arc. S, Ch;   wolde to ryven S;
577) holde] helde S;   spake] speeke S;   a worde no] no worde D, Th;
not a word W, Arc. S;   not oon word S;   578) and] his S;   579) gan]
gonnen S;   myn] his D;   reyn] to reyne Arc. S;   581) That] while S;
languysshing] languysshe W;   sangvissshing B;   his] f. S, Arc. S, Ch, Th;
her T.

84.

And al this w[h]ile my-self I kep[te] close
Amonge the bowes, and my-self gun*n*e hide,
Til at the last the woful man arose,   584
And to a logge went[e] ther besyde,
Wher al the May his custom was to abide,
Sole to compleyn of his peynes kene,
Fro yer to yer vnder the bowes grene.   588

85.

And for be-cause that hit drowe to the nyght,
And that the sun*n*e his arke divrnall
I-passed was, so that his p*er*saunt lyght,
His bryght[e] bemes. and his stremes all   592
*Were in the wawes of the water fall,
Vnder the bordure of our occean,
His chare of golde his course so swyftly ran.

86.

And while the twilyght and the rowes rede   596
Of Phebus lyght wer deaurat a-lyte,
A penne I toke and gan me fast[e] spede,
The woful pleynt of this man to write,
Worde be worde, as he dyd endyte,   600
Lyke as I herde, and coude him tho reporte,
I haue her set, your hertis to dysporte.

87.

Iff oght be mys, leyth the wite on me,
For I am worthy for to bere the blame,   604
Yf eny thing mys-reported be,

---

582) this] the P;   583) bowes] leues Ch;   gunne] ganne
D, gan W, can I S;   585) a] *f.* Ch;   586) to abide] tabide S,
Th; to bide B, Arc. S;   588) bowes] leues P, Ch;   589) be-cause] the
cause Arc. S, Ch;   the] *f.* D, S;   590) that] *f.* P;   591) I-passed]
Passed W;   his] *f.* P;   593) *Were] Wher F, P;   fall] y-fall T;
595) swyftly] swythely T;   596) the²] *f.* W;   598) A penne I toke]
I toke a penne Ch;   spede] to spede S;   599) pleynt] compleynt Arc. S;
peyne P. D;   600) Worde] Right worde S;   dyd] can T;   601 tho] to
Arc. S, Ch;   þer S;   602) to] in Arc. S, Ch;   603) mys] amysse W;   leyth]
ley T, P, D, Th, Arc. S, Ch, W;   ley ye S;   wite] faute W;   604) for¹] *f.* D;
605) mys-reported] amysse-reported S, W.

To make this dite for to seme lame
Thro myn vnkyn*n*yng, but for to seme the same
Lyke as this man his co*m*pleynt did exp*r*esse   608
I axe mercie and foryeuenesse.

88.

And as I wrote me thoght I sawe aferre,
Fer in the west lustely appere
Esperus, the goodly bryght[e] sterre,   612
So glad, so feire, so p*er*saunt eke of chere,
I mene Venus with her bemys clere,
That heuy hertis oonly to releve
Is wont of custom for to shew at eve.   616

89.

And I as fast fel dovn on my kne,
And euen thus to her I gan to preie:
O lady Venus! so feire vpon to se,
Let not this man for his trouthe dey,   620
For that joy thou haddest when thou ley
With Mars thi knyght, *when Vulcan*us* [yow] founde
And with a cheyne vnvisible yow bounde,

90.

To-gedre both tweyne in the same while,   624
That al the court above celestial,
At youre shame gan laughe and smyle.
O feire lady! wel-willy founde at al,
Comfort to carefull! *o goddesse imm*ortal!   628
Be helpyng now, and do thy diligence,
To let the stremes of thin influence

---

606) seme] feyne W;   607) seme] seyne Th, W;   sey P, D, S;
609) axe] ask ȝow Arc.S; *strophe 88—93 f. in* S;   611) Fer in] Vnto
Arc.S; Into Ch; 617) dovn] adoun T, P, D, Th;   618) thus to her] to
hir thus Arc.S, Ch; I gan] gan I Th; to²] *f.* Ch;   649) to se] the se
Arc.S, Ch;   622) *when] whom F, B, W; quhen þat Arc.S, Ch; yow *nur*
in T;   623) cheyne] reyne W;   624) tweyne] twei B, Th, two W;
625) above] aboute W;   626) laughe] for to laugh Arc.S, Ch;   627) O]
A T, P, Arc.S; Ah Th; wel] *f.* Th; willy] wyllynge W;   628) *o]
of F;   629) thy] *f.* P;   630) the] thi P; thin] this P.

91.

Descende dovne, in furtheryng of the trouthe,
Namely of hem that *lye in sorow[e] bounde;   632
Shew now thy myght, and on her wo haue routhe
Er fals Daunger sle hem and confounde:
And specialy let thy myght be founde
For to socour, what so that thou may,   636
The trew[e] man, that in the erber lay.

92.

And al[le] trew[e] further for his sake,
O glad[e] sterre! o lady Venus myn!
And [cause] his lady him to grace take;   640
Her hert of stele to mercy so enclyne,
Er that thy bemes go vp to declyne,
And er that thou now go fro vs adovne,
For that love thou haddest to Adoun.   644

93.

And when she was goon to her rest
I rose anon, and home to bed[de] went
For werry wery, me thoght hit for the best,
Preyng thus in al my best entent,   648
That al[le] trew[e], that be with daunger shent,
With mercie may, in réles of her peyn,
Recured be, er May come eft aye[y]n.

94.

And for that I ne may noo lenger wake,   652
Farewel ye louers al[le] that be trewe!

---

631) the] thy Arc. S, Ch;   632) *lye] he F; lyeth P; be S, Arc. S, Ch;
633) on] of Arc. S, Ch; wo] sorow T;   634) Er] Theyr W; hem] hym P,
Arc. S;   635) be] *f*. P;   636) that] *f*. Ch;   637) The] Thi Ch;   638) alle]
the D;   further] men thou furthir Ch;   639) glade] goodly Arc. S, Ch;
640) cause] *f*. F;   grace] hir grace Arc. S;   take] call B;   642) thy]
the Ch; vp] *f*. D;   643) now go] go now Arc. S, Ch;   644) thou] þat thou
Arc. S;   Adoun] Adomoun D, down W;   645) when] quhen þat Arc. S, Ch;
to] unto Arc. S, Ch;   646) went] I went P, Arc. S.;   647) werry wery] verily
Arc. S, Ch; very T, P, D, Th; hit] hit was T, P;   648) thus] ryght thus
Arc. S;   649) trewe] true louers W;   650) may in relese] thou relese P;
651) Recured] Recouered P, D, Arc. S, Ch; eft] *f*. P;   652) And] *f*. P;
ne] *f*. P, D, S, Arc. S, Ch, W;   may] may now Arc. S;   noo] not no P;
653) Farewel] Fareþe wel S; al] *f*. P.

Prayng to God, and thus my leve I take,
That er the sunne to morowe be ryse newe,
And er he haue ayen his rosen hewe,   656
That eche of yow may haue such a grace,
His owne lady in armes to embrace.

95.

I mene thus, that in al honeste,
With-oute more ye may to-gedre speke,   660
What-so yow list at good liberte,
That eche may to other her hert[e] breke,
On Jelosie oonly to be wreke,
That hath so louge of *malice and envie   664
Werred Trouthe with his tiranye.

96. L'envoye

Princes, pleseth hit [to] your benignite
This litil Dite [for] to haue in mynde
Of womanhede also for to se,   668
Your trew[e] man may summe mercie fynde,
And Pite eke, that longe hath [be] behynde,
Let [him] ayein be prouoked to grace;
For by my trouthe hit is ayen[e]s kynde,   672
Fals Daunger to occupie his place.

97. L'envoye du quaer.

*Go litel quayre, go vnto my lyves quene
And my verry hertis souereigne,

---

654) leve] lyue W;   655) be] f. P;   to morowe be ryse] be rysen
to morowe S;   656) er] as S;   he] ȝe T;   haue] haþe S;   his] f. T, P, Th,
Arc. S;   658) thus] ryght thus Arc. S;   that] f. T, P, D, Th, S, Ch, W;
660) ye] you T;   to - gedre] wíth othir Arc. S;   661) yow] ye Th;
662) eche] eueryche S;   to] tyl Ch;   herte] hertys T, S;   663) On] of S;
Jelosie] jelosies T, P, D, Th, S;   oonly] and S;   to] for to S, Arc. S, Ch;   be
wreke] beon awreke S,   bilwreke W;   664) *malice] his malice F, D, Th,
Arc. S, Ch;   666) strophenüberschrift L'envoye] f. T, P, D, Arc. S, Ch;
pleseth] plese S;   hit] f. Arc. S;   to] f. F, B, W;   your] you of your T;
667) for] nur in P, Arc. S;   mynde] your mynde S;   668) also] oonly S;
669) Your] That ȝour Arc. S;   trewe] f. D, Th;   summe] f. W;   your Th;
670) longe hath be] hath be long P;   hath long ben Arc. S, Ch;   be] f. F;
671) Let] That Arc. S, Ch;   him] f. F, B, W;   be prouoked] prouoked by S;
be promited D;   672) by my trouthe] trewily Arc. S;   673) to] for to
Arc. S;   674) strophenüberschrift L'envoye du quaer] f. T, P, D, Th, S,
Arc. S, Ch;   *Go] So F, T;   goᵒ] f. P, D, Th;   vnto] to P, S, Arc. S, Ch;
675) my] f. D;   to my Arc. S, Ch.

And be ryght glad for she shal the sene; 676
Such is thi grace, but I, alas, in peyne
Am left behinde and not to whom to pleyn;
For Mercie, Routhe, Grace, and eke Pite
Exiled be, that I may not ateyne, 680
Recure to fynde of *myn adversite.

---

676) for] for þat Arc. S; shal] hath D; 677) Suche] Sche D; thi]
the P; 678) left] lest T, B; and] bnt B, W; to pleyn] me pleyne S;
complayn D; to complene P, W; 679) Routhe] trouthe W; 681) Recure]
Recouer D, S, Arc. S, Ch; *myn] hym F.

Anmerkungen.

1) Flora .... quene] vgl. *Chorl and Bird* s. 180 (Halliwell Lydgate's
M. P). Of flowres also Flora goddes and quene
Story of Thebes, Prolog 13 ff.:

When that Flora the noble mightie quene
The soile hath clad in newe tender grene.

Secreta Secretorum 1377: ..... flora that is of floures quene.
the fresshe lusti quene] vgl. *Temple of Glas* 93: þe lusti fresshe quene.
3 u. 4) Phebus ... amyd the Bole] vgl. *Troilus* II, 50 ff.

In May that Moder is of monthes gladde
That fresshe floures blew, and white, and rede
By quyke agayne, that wynter dede made
And ful of bawme is fletynge every mede:
When Phebus dothe his bryghte bemes sprede
Ryght in the white Bole, it so bytyde
As I shal synge ...

Story of Phebes, Prolog 1 f.: Whan bright[e] Phebus passed was the ram
Midde of April and into bulle cam.
Edmund, Zusatz zu buch III, 234: .... whan the sonne shene
I-entrid was into the boolys hede.
Flower and Leaf. 1 ff.: When that Phebus his chaire of gold so hie
Had*d*e whirled up the sterry sky alofte
And in the bole was entred certainly.
5—9) Lucifer] vgl. *Isop* (hggb. v. Zupitza, *Archiv* 85) v. 72 ff.:
But sluggy hertys out of þeyr slepe to wake
When Lucifer toward þe dawnyng
Lawgeth in þe oryent *and* haþe þe west forsake
To chace awey þe myghty clowdys blake.
Temple of Gl. 253: And Lucifer to voide þe nyȝtes sorow
In clerenes passeþ erli bi þe morow.
Flour of Courtesie 115. And Lucifer amonge the skyes donne
A morowe sheweth, to voide nightes tene.

Story of Thebes (nach Schick *T. of Gl.* Aumerk. 253):
.... Lucifer the sterre
Gladeth the morowe at his vprising.

8 u. 9) vgl. *Temple of Gl.* 330: Cheif recounford after þe blak nyȝt
To voide woful oute of her heuynes.

12) with sainte John to borowe] borowe ist hier substantiv; to borowe
= zum Bürgen vgl. *Complaint of Mars* 9, *Squyeres Tale* 596, *Isle of Ladies*
2048, *Kingis Quair* 59, 6. Gower's *Confessio Amantis* (ed. Pauly Bd. II,
s. 241) Lyndsay's *Dream* 996; *Troil.* II 1524: Venus to borwe; *Ralph Roister
Doister* (ed. Dodsley-Hazlitt III 141, z. 8 v. unten) & Feylde's *Controversy
between a lover & a Jay*: Saint-George to borowe; Spenser in *Shepherd's
Calender, May*: by my dear borowe (= Christus); vgl. auch Irving, *History
of Scotish Poetry* s. 136 und note ³, der noch weitere beispiele giebt.

12) Hope] Personification aus *Rom. of the Rose* 2754 u. ö.

13) Daunger] vgl. *Rom. of the Rose* 1524 u. ö., *Prolog z. Leg. of g. W.*
160; *Parl. of Foul.* 136, *Troil.* II 1376, *Merciles Beauté* 16, *Court of Love*
831; *Temple of Gl.* 156 vgl. Schick's anmerk. dazu.

Dispeyre] vgl. *Court of L.* 1036: The lovers foe, that cleped is Dispaire. Ferner *Cuckow & Nightingale* 176; zu dem disput zwischen Hope
und Dispaire vgl. *Court of L.* 1046 f:
.... than came Hope and seid, "My frende let be!
Beleve him not: Despaire he gynneth dote."

17) vgl. *Parl. of Foul.* 496: .... I mote for sorwe deye
Troil. IV 404: But Troilus that neigh for sorwe deyde.

28) persaunt] ausserdem noch v. 358, 591, 613. Chaucer gebraucht
dafür piercing vgl. Skeat *On the Romant of the Rose* (in der introduction
p. XC seiner ausgabe der *Prioresses Tale* etc. Clarendon Press). Lydgate
verwendet das wort häufig, vgl. Schick's anmerkung zu *Temple of Gl.* 328.

29) Had dried up] vgl. *Guy of Warwick* (ed. Zupitza Wiener Sitzungsberichte Bd. 74) 32. 4: Or that the sunne with his feruent hete
Hath on the levys dryed up the weete.

ähnl. stellen: *Knightes P.* 635 ff.; *Legend of Thisbe* 69.

31) vgl. *Troye Book* (nach Warton-Hazlitt III, s. 84):
And floures eke agayn the morow tyde
Upon their stalkes gan playn their leves wide.

34) golde-borned] goldglänzend *borned* part. zu *bornen, burnen* (afrz.
burnir) polieren, glänzend machen; jetzt wird dafür das vom selben stamm
abgeleitete *burnish* gebraucht.

House of Fame 1384: As burned gold hyt shoon to see.

Fraunkel. Tale 511: (Phebus) schon as the burned gold with stremes bright.

Gower's *Confessio* (ed. Pauli Bd. II 272): Whose flees of burned gold was all.

Life of our Lady (nach Warton-Hazlitt III s. 58):
(Phebus) ... his wayne gold-yborned

Legend of Daun Joss (Ldgate's *M. P.*, Halliwell s. 65): lettris of burned gold

Troye Book (nach Wart.-Halzlitt III s. 89:
... the gold that was burned bright.

36) ryuer .:. costey] vgl. *Rom of the Rose* 134:
The ryver syde costeiyng.

37) berel or cristal] vgl. *Chorl and Bird* s. 183:
And the pynacles of biralle and cristale.
Troye Book (nach Wart.-Hazlitt III s. 89): .... and eche fenestrall
Wrought were of beryl and of cleare crystall.
40) in compas rounde] vgl. *Rom. of the Rose* 4183:
The tour was rounde maad in compas.
Albon I 358.   In compas rounde and large.
42) walled with grene stoon] vgl. *Parl. of Foul.* 122:
Ryght of a parke walled with grene stoon
March. Tale 785: He had a gardyn walled al with stoon.
45) ... al the wode rong] vgl. *Book of the Duch.* 311:
For al my chamber gan to rynge
Chorl and Bird s. 182: ... al the gardeyne of the noyse rong
Kingis Quair 35. 5: ... all the gardyng and the wallis rong.
47) vgl. *Rom. of the Rose* 78: Than doth the nyghtyngale hir myght.
Flower and Leaf 435 f.: For then the nightingale, that al the day
Had in the laurer sete, and did her might
The whole service to singe ...
52) celured ... with bowys grene] celured = überwölbt; vgl. *Troye Book* (nach Wart.-Hazl. III s. 92): Embowed over al the work to cure
So marveylous was the celature.
ähnl. *Troil.* II 821: And shadwed wel with blosmy bowes grene.
57) findet sich fast wörtlich in *Pur le Roy* Str. 3 wieder:
The ayre attempred, the wyndes smowth and playn.
eyre atempre vgl. *Parl. of Foul.* 204, *Book of the D* 341, *Isle of Ladies* 1201.
59) Lies: So hólsom wás and só norsshíng he kynde.
64) Daphene] Ihre verwandlung in einen lorbeerbaum siehe *Knightes Tale* 1204 ff.: Ther saugh I Dane yturned til a tre
I mene nought the goddesse Dyane
But Penneus doughter, which that highte Dane.
Troil. III 677: O Phebus! thynke when Dane hire-selven shette
Vnder the barke and laurer wax for drede.
Temple of Gl. 115: ... Daphne vnto a laurer tre
Iturned was when she did fle.   Vgl. auch Schick's anmerkung dazu.
64—74) Aehnliche baumaufzählungen siehe in *Rom. of the Rose* 1379, *Parl. of Foul.* 176, *Knight. Tale* 2063; Spencer's *Faerie Queen* Book I, Canto I. strophe.
68) philbert] siehe Gower's *Confessio* Bd. II s. 30:
... Phillis in the same throwe
Was shape into a nute tre,
That alle men it mighte se;
And after Phillis philliberd
This tre was cleped in the yerd.
Temple of Gl. 89: ... she was honged vpon a filbert tre; zur geschichte von Phyllis und Demophon siehe *Legend of Phyllis*, *Book of the Duch.* 728, *House of F* 388, *Man of Lawe's Prolog* 65; ferner Schick in der anmerkung zu *Temple of Gl.* 86—90 und Holthausen, Anglia XVI, s. 264.

77) ... under an hille] vgl. *Rom. of the R.* 114 f.:

> For from an hille that stood ther ner
> Cam doun the streme ful stif and bold.

78) The grauel golde] vgl. *Troye Book* (nach Wart.-Haz. III s. 84):

> the grauel and the bryght stone
> As any gold agayne the sonne shone.

Kingis Quair 152. 4: the grauel bryght as ony gold
Gower's *Confessio* Bd. II s. 137: The grauel with the smale stones

> To gold thei torne both atones.

80) vgl. *Troye Book* (nach Wart.-Haz. III, s. 85):

> And softe as veluet was the yonge grene

Rom of the R. 1417 ff.: Aboute the brynkes of these welles

> And by the stremes over al elles
> Sprange up the gras as thicke yset
> And softe as any velvet.

87) Narcissus] Seine liebesgeschichte ist ausführlich erzählt in *Rom. of the R.* 1469 ff. und in Gower's *Confessio* Bd. I s. 199 ff. zu unserer stelle vgl. besonders *Rom. of the R.* 1616:

> For Venus sone, daun Cupido
> Hath sowne there of love the seed,
> That help ne. lith ther noon, ne rede,
> So cerclith it the welle aboute.

90) Ich möchte die lesart *hide* gegenüber der auch von Morris in seiner ausgabe der *Compl. of the Bl. Kn.* (Chaucer, Aldine Edit. Bd. VI) angenommenen lesart *abide* aufrecht erhalten, da der sinn doch wohl der ist, dass Cupido die todbringende saat (the greyn of deth) auf so geheime weise versteckt hielt (so covertely dide hide), dass ein jeder, der aus der genannten quelle, deren wasser man sich durch den duft der pflanzen vergifset denken muss, trinkt, dem tode verfallen ist.

94. 95) vgl. Gower's *Confessio* Bd. I s. 53:

> Amid the plaine he saw a welle
> So faire there might no man telle
> In which Dyane naked stood
> To bathe and play her in the flood
> With many a nimphe which her serveth.

97) Acteon] vgl. *Knight Tale* 1206 ff.:

> Ther saugh I Acteon an hert i-maked,
> For vengance that he saugh Dyane al naked;
> I saugh how that his houndes han him caught
> And freten him, for that they knew him naught.

ferner Gower's *Confessio* Bd. I, s. 54.

99) Das durch Morris eingeschobene *of* habe ich nirgends belegt gefunden.

102) pensifhede] vgl. *Temple of Gl.* 2. For pensifhede and for high distress. Vgl. auch Sckick's anmerkung dazu.

122) delytable place] vgl. *Fraunkel. Tale* 171:

> and eek in other places delytables.

124) vgl. *Parl. of F.* 229: Her names shul noght here be told for me.

125) erber] vgl. *Prolog* zu *Leg. of g. W.* 203 ff.:
>   And in a litel herber that I have
>   That benched was on turves fressh ygrave
>   I had men sholde me my couche make.

vgl. auch *Flower and Leaf* 49 ff.

127) floures ynde] *ynde* ist hier adjektiv (< afrz. inde) und bedeutet *blau, indigo* (die aus Indien gekommene farbe). Vgl. *Cursor Mundi* 9920:
>   þe toþer hew next to fynde
>   Is al blew men callen ynde.

Rom. of the R. 67: ... flouris ynde and pers.
Chorl and Bird s. 190: saphires that shewethe colour Inde
>   „   „   „   s. 188: saphires or other stones hynde.
Court of L. 78: no saphir Ind.

129) hulfere] an. hulfr. = Stechpalme.
wodebynde] ne. woodbine, Geissblatt. Vgl. *Knightes Tale* 650:
>   To maken him a garland of the greves
>   Were it of woodebynde or hawethorne leves.

130) vgl. *Book of the D.* 404: ... so at the laste
>   I was war of a man in blak.

131) Man kann hier zweifelhaft sein, wie das komma zu setzen ist, da *colour* sowohl zu *blake and white,* als auch zu *pale and wan* gezogen werden kann.

138) Des metrums wegen und auch weil lieblingswort Lydgate's habe ich die von Arc. S, Ch vertretenen lesart *constreint* der von den übrigen hs. u. dr. vertretenen lesart *constreynyng* vorgezogen. Ueber das vorkommen dieses wortes siehe Schick's anmerkung zu *Temple of Gl.* 2 u. 11.

151) fortune and ... eure] eure (< afrz. ëure, lat. augurium); vgl.
Court of L. 634: my fortune and my ure
Kingis Quair 10. 2: .. my fortune and vre.

154) vgl. *Troil.* IV. 1184: .... of swough she therwith brayde
Squyeres Tale 469: And after that she gan of swown abreyde.
Wife of Bath's Prologue 799: ... out of my swogh I breyde.

163) by good proporcioun] vgl. *Temple of Gl.* 277:
>   egalli bi good proporcioun
Troil. V 828: and complet formed by proporcioun.

164) delyver strengthe] delyver (< afz. delibre) = flink. Vgl. *Prolog* der *Cant.-T.* 83: of his stature he was of even lengthe
>   And wonderly delyver and grete of strengthe.

165) Gruffe] (< an. ā grufu (ligja)) mit dem gesichte auf dem boden liegend. Vgl. *Knight. Tale* 91: they fillen gruf, and criden pitously.
>   *Prior. Tale* 223, And gruf he fil al plat upon the grounde.

168) awhaped and amate] = verzagt und niedergeschlagen; vgl. *Troil.* I 316; all awhaped; *Anelida* 215: awhaped countenauce; *Leg. of Philomela* 94: afered and whaped; *Temple of Gl.* 401: þei ... were waped and amate; siehe auch Schick's anmerkung dazu.

178) O Nyobe ..] ähnliche invocationen finden sich auch in andern werken Lydgate's, vgl. Schick's anmerkung zu *Temple of Gl.* 961.

180) woful Mirre] vgl. *Troil.* IV 110:

> So bittre teres wepe noughte as I fynde
> The woful Myrra, through the bark and rynde.

181) my honde eke quake] vgl. *Troil.* III 1784:

> And now my penne alas, with which I write
> Quaketh for drede of that I most endite.

Lydgate's *Application to the Duke of Glowester for money* (Halliwell, M. P.) s. 49: .... whan I wrote my hand felt I quake
bei Lydgate findet sich diese phrase sehr oft, vgl. Schick's anmerkung zu *Temple of Gl.* 947.

183 ff.) Aehnlich in *Troil.* I 12:

> For wel it sit, the sothe for to seyne
> A woful wight to han a drery face
> And to a sorwful tale a sory chere.

190) vgl. *Temple of Gl.* 822: My witt is dull ...; *Legend of Austin* (Halliwell. s. 149) ... I am of wittes dull; *Court of L.* 151: My witte is dull and hard; Gower's *Confessio* II s. 23: And eke my wittes ben so dulle.

191) vgl. *Temple of Gl.* 951: I want connyng, his peynes to discryve und ähnlich *Troil.* V 267 ff.

208) vgl. *Anelida* 262: Your manly resoun oght it to respite

> To slene your frende, and namely me
> That never yet in no degre
> Offended yow, ...

215) sehr häufige Formel, vgl. *Troil.* II 1306:

> (Troilus) That lay, as dose thes lovers in a traunce.

Lydgate's *Testament* (Halliwell s. 242) Whyl that I lay compleyning in a traunce; ferner *Troil.* IV 314; *Monkes Tale* 725; *Complaint* 525 (Appendix I in Schick's *Temple of Gl.*) etc.

218 ff.) vgl. hiermit den anfang des *Parl. of F.*

225) Die änderung von *grounde* in *bounde*, wie sie Arc. S. und darnach Morris vorgenommen, ist nicht nötig, da *grounde* hier einen ganz guten sinu giebt, wenn als particip zu *grinden* (= bedrücken, quälen) aufgefasst.

228) feble and feynt] vgl. *Edmund* III 80:

> My spirit fehle and feynt.

229) vgl. *Fall's of Pr.* 124 a (aus Schick's anmerk. zu *Temple of Gl.* 358):

> With loves axesse now wer thei whote now cold

Launcelot (ed. Skeat) l. 30: So he the morowe set I was a-fyre

> In felinge of the acces hot and cold

Cuckow and Nightingale 38 f.: Yet have I felte of that sekenes in May

> Both hote and colde, an access every day.

230 u. 231) vgl. *Complaint* 531 (Appendix I in *Temple of Gl.*)

> Of hasty cold and sodeyn hete
> Now I cheuere and now I suete.

233) vgl. *Troil.* I, 420: For hete of cold, for cold of hete I dye, und ähnlich in Gower's *Confessio* III, s. 9: In colde I brenne and frese in hete. Vgl. auch Schick's anmerkung zu *Complaint* 529.

237) Gegen die von den hs. und dr. vertretene lesart *colde* ist die von Thynne und auch von Morris angenommene *-hete-* jedenfalls die richtige; vgl. *Troil.* I, 120.

241) *This ys* ist in *this'* zusammenzuziehen und der vers mit doppeltem auftakt zu lesen. ·

248) with hert and all] vgl. *Rom. of the R.* 1883:
> To serve his love with hert and all.

Temple of Gl. 991: That hert and al, withoute strife, ar yolde.

257) Envye] Personification aus dem *Rom. of the R.* 248 u. ö. Gower's *Confessio* I, s. 159; prolog zu *Leg. of g. W.* 358; *Court of L.* 1254; *Temple of Gl.* 147; vgl. Schick's anmerk. dazu.

259) Trouthe] vgl. *Piers Plowman* C. text IX, 137 u. ö.; Gower's *Confessio* I, s. 333; *Compl. to Pite* 74; *Good Counseil of Chaucer* 7; *Ballade sent to king Rickard* 15; King James' *Good Counsel* 5, *Pur le Roy* (Halliwell) s. 12.

260) Malebonche] bekannte figur im *Rom. de la R.* (die engl. übersetzung hat Wikked-Tonge 3027 u. ö.); Gower's *Confessio* I, s. 159; *Flower and Leaf* 580.

263) Fals-suspecioun] siehe *Rom. of the R.* 2507; *Maunciple Tale* 173, *Temple of Gl.* 153.

277) Cruelte] vgl. *Compl. to Pite* 11 u. ö.

285) vgl. *Man of Lawes Tale* 715 f.:
> O mygthy God, if that it be thy wille
> Seth thou art rightful jugge, how may this be
> That thou wolt suffre innocentz to spille
> And wikked folk regne in prosperite.

Knightes Tale 455: What governaunce is in this prescience
> That gilteles tormenteth innocence.

288) vgl. *Anelida* 314: Almighty god, of throuthe the sovereign.

290) loves firy cheyn] vgl. *Temple of Gl.* 574:
> But now of nwe within his fire cheyn
> I am embraced.

295) vgl. *Temple of Gl.* 367: O lady Venus consider and see.

St. Margar. 338: When I considre withynne myself and se.

Secreta Secretor. 1160: ... consider also and se.

sight] vgl. *Isop* 289. I se hit well in myn inward sight.

302) vre < afrz. uevre, lat. opera; noch erhalten in ne. inure (aus in ure).

316) vgl. *Anelida* 224: For I loved one with al my hert and myght.

317) vgl. *Troil.* V, 1319: With herte, body, lif, lust, thought and all.

328 u. 329) vgl. Gower's *Confessio* I, 216:
> Thus stood trouth under the charge
> And the falshed goth at large.

to go at large (large, als substantiv) ist eine häufige formel. Vgl. *Wife of Bath's Prologue* 322, *Chorl and Bird* s. 184 und 189. Lydgate's *Testament* s. 225.

330) Palamides] gemeint ist hier nicht Palamedes, sohn des Nauplius, der im trojanischen kriege eine hervorragende rolle spielt, und auch von Lydgate in seinem *Troye Book* und den *Falls of Princes* angeführt wird, sondern Palamides the Sarrasin, ein ritter aus dem Arthursagenkreis, dessen thaten und vergebliches werben um Isolde in dem prosaroman

von *Tristan* erzählt werden und danach von Malory im 8., 9. und 10. buche
seines *Morte Arthure* (vgl. Sommer's ausgabe von Malory's werk, bd. III,
s. 9 und 278 ff.). Als ritter der tafelrunde wird Palamides auch in einem
griechischen gedichte aus dem XII. jahrh. (?) erwähnt, das von Francisque
Michel: *Tristan, Recueil de ce qui reste des Poèmes relatifs à ses aventures
composés en françois en anglo-normand et en grec dans les XII et XIII
siècles.* London 1835 in bd. 2, s. 269 unter dem titel: „Poema graecum de
rebus gestis regis Arturi, Tristani, Lanceloti, Galbani, Palamedis, aliorum-
que equitum tabulae rotundae" veröffentlicht wurde.

344—57) Ercules] seine thaten sind erzählt in den *Monkes Tale* 105 ff.,
zu unserer stelle vgl. bes. v. 127 ff.:

At bothe the worldes endes, saith Trophee,
In stede of boundes, he a piler sette.

Gower's *Confessio* II, s. 70: This knight the two pillers of bras,
The whiche yet a man may finde,
Set up in the desert of Ynde
That was the worthy Hercules.

346) findet sich fast wörtlich in *Reason and Sensualite*:
That was of strengthe pereles;
vgl. Schick's anmerkungen zu *Temple of Gl.* 787, wo auch die übrigen
stellen zu Hercules' liebe zu Dejanira aufgezählt sind.

354) vgl. *Troil.* I, 317: he may goon in the daunce
of hem that Love list febly for to avaunce.

356) Morris' lesart *not stryve* ist unmöglich, denn der infin. *stryve*
kann nicht reimen mit *lif*; auch der sinn der stelle verlangt notwendiger-
weise das subst. *strif.*

358—64) Phebus] seine liebesgeschichten sind erzählt in Gower's *Confessio* bd. I, s. 305 und 336; *Maunciples Tale*; *Troil.* I, 659 ff.; siehe auch
Schick's anmerk. zu *Temple of Gl.* 112—116.

359) vgl. *Maunciples Tale* 1:
When Phebus dwelt her in this erth adoun.

365) Piramus] vgl. *Legend. of Thisbe*; *Parl of F.* 289; *March. Tale*
884; Gower's *Confessio* bd. I, s. 325; III, s. 360; *Temple of Gl.* 81 (vgl.
auch Schick's anmerk. dazu).

366) Tristram] vgl. *Parl. of F.* 240; prolog zu *Leg. of g. W.* 254;
Balade to Rosemunde 20; Gower's *Confessio* bd. III, s. 17 u. 359; *Temple
of Gl.* 79 (und Schick's anmerk. dazu).

367) Achilles] vgl. *Parl. of F.* 290; prolog zu *Leg. of g. W.* 258;
Book of D. 1067 ff.; Gower's *Confessio* bd. III, s. 360; *Temple of Gl.* 94
(s. Schick's anmerk. dazu).

Antonyus] vgl. *Legend of Cleopatra*; *Court of L.* 873; Gower's *Confessio* bd. III, s. 362; *Temple of Gl.* 778 (s. Schick's anmerk. dazu).

368) Arcite, Palamoon] vgl. *Knightes Tale*, *Temple of Gl.* 102 ff. (s.
Schick's anmerk. dazu).

him Palamoon] von solchen verbindungen von pronomen + eigennamen gibt Schick *Temple of Gl.* anmerk. zu v. 81 eine reihe von belegen.

372 u. 373) Jason und Mede] vgl. *Legend of Hypsipyle and Mede*;
prolog zu *Leg. of g. W.* 266; *Book of D.* 330; *House of F.* 401; *Squyeres*

Tale 548; *Man of Lawes Prologue* 72 f.; Gower's *Confessio* bd. II, s. 236; III, s. 361; *Temple of Gl.* 62, 63 (s. Schick's anmerk. dazu).

374) Da ich der hs. F folge, so habe ich Tereus beibehalten, obwohl auch die durch die übrigen hs. und dr. vertretene lesart Theseus mit gleichem recht gesetzt werden kann.

Tereus] vgl. *Legend of Philomene*; *Troil.* II, 64 ff.; Gower's *Confessio* bd. II, s. 314; Skeat's note zu *Kingis Quair* 55; Schick's anmerkung zu *Temple of Gl.* 97—99.

Theseus] vgl. *Legend of Ariadne*; *House of F.* 403 ff.; Gower's *Confessio* bd. II, s. 303.

375 Ene] vgl. *Legend of Dido*; *House of F.* 240; *Book of D.* 732 f.; *Man of Lawes Prologue* 64; *Court of L.* 232; Gower's *Confessio* bd. II, s. 4; *Temple of Gl.* 58 (s. Schick's anmerk. zu 55—61).

379) fals Arcite] vgl. *Anelida and Arcite*; *Court of L.* 235.

380) Demophon] vgl. *Legend of Phyllis*; *House of F.* 388; *Book of D.* 728; *Man of Lawes Prologue* 65; Gower's *Confessio* bd. II, s. 26; *Temple of Gl.* 87 (s. Schick's anmerk. zu 86—90).

eke ist, wie auch öfter bei Chaucer, zweisilbig zu lesen.

386, 87) Adon] vgl. *Troil.* III, 671:

> For love of hym that lovedest in the shawe
> I mene Adon, that with the bore was slawe.

Knightes Tale 1366; *Temple of Gl.* 64 (s. Schick's anmerk. dazu).

393—99) Ipomones und Athalant] die geschichte, wie Ipomenes Atalanta dadurch erwarb, dass er sie im wettlaufe besiegte, wird ausführlich erzählt von Ovid *Metam.* X, 560 ff.; und auch in den *Heroiden* im briefe Paris' an Helena wird ihrer erwähnung gethan. Chaucer erwähnt Atalante im *House of F.* 286.

401 ff.) Eine ähnliche stelle ist *Troil.* V, 1842 und 1866.

404) suerde of sorowe] vgl. *Anelida* 272:

> And of me rekke not a myte
> Thogh the suerde of sorow byte
> My woful herte, thro your cruelte.

Anelida 215: The suerde of sorowe, ywhet with fals plesaunce.

410 ff.) vgl. *St. Edmund* I, 113:

> Fredam, bounte, manhod, nor gentilesse
> Prowesse in armis, nor sheltrouns in bataile —
> Withoute grace what may all this auaile?

412) vgl. Gower's *Confessio* II, s. 56:

> great travaile in straunge londes.

413) vgl. *St. Edmund* I, 254: may litil or nought availe.

416) grete emprises] vgl. *Fraunkel. Tale* 4:

> And many a labour, and many a grete emprise
> He for his lady wrought er she was wonne.

419) inpartyng] von den schreibern fälschlich in partyng gelesen. s. Skeat, *Academy* 1896. I. p. 512.

426) cured ist die richtige Lydgate'sche form; Morris' änderung in covred ist unnötig.

432—33) vgl. *Rom. of the R.* 2540:

> They be so double in hir falshede
> For they in herte cunne thenke a thing
> And seyn another in hir spekyng.

434) vgl. *Temple of Gl.* 168:
> Thurgh whos falsnes hindred be the trewe.

447—48) Morris' lesarten habe ich nirgends belegt gefunden. Seine änderungen sind unnötig, da die stelle, so wie sie ist, einen ganz guten sinn giebt.

448) vgl. *Anelida* 237: Ryght as him list, he laugheth at my peyn.

449) vgl. *Fraunkel. Tale* 310: Lo, Lord! my lady hath my deth y-sworne Withouten gilt.

461—462) Lydgate hat sich hier eine sehr auffällige assonanz zu schulden kommen lassen, die sich vielleicht dadurch erklären lässt, dass sich ihm das bild des particip *wenende* und des verbalsubstantivs *wenyng* mischte. Die zweite, auch von Morris angenommene lesart *as he wende* halte ich für unrichtig.

469) Aehnliche klagen über Cupido's ungerechtigkeit vgl. Gower's *Confessio* bd. II, s. 59, *Cuckow and Nightingale* 197.

470) *this is* ist in *this'* zusammenzuziehen wie in v. 241.

478) vgl. *Anelida* 242: Unto my fo, that yafe my hert a wounde.

484) sehr häufig vorkommende phrase. Vgl. bes. *Troil.* V, 1276 f.:
> Alas the while that I was borne.

488) vgl. *Guy of Warwick* 24, 2:
> By parcas sustren was sponne my lyves threde!

Troil. III, 684: O fatal sustren! which er any cloth
> Me shapen was, my desteyne me sponne.

Knightes Tale 708: That shapen was my deth er that my shert.

491 ff.) vgl. *Parl. of F.* 379: Nature the vicaire of thalmyghty lorde.

Pour le Roy s. 6: The ffirst of hem callyd was Nature
> As sche that hathe under her demeyne
> Man, best, and foule, and every creature.

Lydgate's *Testament* s. 243 (Nature) Which is of Ver callyd cheef pryncesse
> And undyr God ther worldly emperesse.

Weitere belege s. Schick's einleitung zu *Temple of Gl.* p. CXXIV f.

495) vgl. *Doktoures Tale* 9:
> For Nature hath with sovereign diligence
> I formed hir in so gret excellence.

497) Daunger to guyde] vgl. *Court of L.* 129 f.:
> The king had Daunger ner to him standyng
> The Quene of Love Disdeyn.

Court of L. 831: Ther was no lak, sauf Daunger had a lyte
> This godely fressh in rule and governaunce.

Parl. of F. 136: Disdeyn and daunger is the guyde.

Gower's *Confessio* I, 331: ... It is a daunger
> which is my ladies counseiller.

511) hasty beleve] vgl. *Chorl and Bird* s. 186:
> Hasty credence hath caused gret hyndryng,

ferner s. 190—91.

512) mordred and sleyn] auf ähnliche phrasen weist Schick in *Temple of Gl.* anmerk. 634 hin.

519) vgl. Gower's *Confessio* bd. I, s. 248:
> And that he shuld algate deie.

544) vgl. *Troil.* v. 412: ... godely, feyre, fresshe may.

554) gruching or rebellioun] eine sehr beliebte phrase Lydgate's, vgl. Schick's anmerk. zu *Temple of Gl.* 424.

558) testament] vgl. *Rom. of the R.* 4609:

> I wol me confesse in good entent
> And make in haste my testament
> As lovers doon, that felen smerte.

568) vgl. *Temple of Gl.* 1129:

> For life nor deþe, for joie ne for peyne.

587) vgl. *Knightes Tale* 214: And to himself compleynyng of his woo.

589) vgl. *St. Edmund* III, 702: ... because it drouh to nyght.

596) vgl. *Troye Book* (nach Warton-Hazlitt III, s. 85):

> Whan that the rowes and the rayes rede
> Estward to vs full early gonnen sprede
> Even at the twelyght in the dawnyng.

598) vgl. *St. Edmund* zusatz zu book III, 239:

> My penne I toke, ffaste gan me speed.

612) Esperus] vgl. *Life of our Lady* (nach Warton-Hazlitt III, s. 58):

> And esperus when that it doth appere.

Temple of Gl. 1343 (s. Schick's anmerk. dazu).

621) Mars und Venus] vgl. *Knightes Tale* 1525 ff.; *Court of L.* 85; Gower's *Confessio* bd. II, s. 148; *Temple of Gl.* 126 ff. (s. Schick's anmerkungen dazu).

625) Ein sehr knapper vers; lies: át youre shámë gán | láugh and smile. (Typus B), der aber durch änderung von *gan* in *gunnë* oder durch einstellung von *to* (gan to) leicht nach Typus A gelesen werden kann.

644) vgl. *Knightes Tale* 1366: For thilke love thou haddest to Adoun.

647) for werry wery] vgl. *Troil.* IV, 678:

> ... she felt almost her herte dye
> For wo and wery of that compagnie.

Ueber ähnliche verbindungen vgl. Schick's anmerk. zu *Temple of Gl.* 632.

648) vgl. *St. Edmund* I, 596: Beseckyng you in al my best entent.

663) Jelousie] personification aus den *Rom. of the R.* 3820 u. ö.; *Parl. of F.* 252; *Troil.* III, 788; V, 1213; *Compl. of Mars and Venus* 331; *Temple of Gl.* 148 (s. Schick's anmerk. dazu).

666) Princes] wer damit gemeint ist, konnte bis jetzt nicht festgestellt werden; in ähnlicher weise beginnt Lydgate das envoy in der *Ballad on the forked head-dresses of ladies,* Halliwell s. 46 ff.:

> Noble princessis, this litel short dyté
> Rudely compiled, lat it be noon offence
> To your womanly mercifell pyté u. s. w.

670) Pite] vgl. *Rom. of the R.* 3501; *Compl. to Pite*; Prolog zu *Leg. of g. W.* 161; *Merciles Beaute* 15; *Balad sent to King Richard*; *Court of L.* 701; *Pur le Roy* Halliwell s. 14.

672) ähnlich in *Compl. to Pite* 89:

> Ye be than fro your heritage y-throwe
> By Cruelte, that occupieth your place.

674) Aehnliche phrasen wurden von Schick, anmerk. 1393 des *Temple of Gl.* zusammengestellt, wozu noch hinzugefügt werden kann *Pur le Roy* s. 45: Go pety quaier.

681) fast wörtlich wiederholt iu *Guy of Warwick* 15. 2. Recure to finde of their adnersite.

Glossar.

abreyde, 15, 153, auffahren, erwachen.
access, 136, 229, fieber.
algate, 519, auf jedeu fall.
amate, 168, niedergeschlagen, ermattet.
asshe, 73, Esche.
astert, 490, entkommen.
aswage, 100, besänftigen.
ateyn, 340, gelangen; 680, erreichen.
avisement, 278, überlegung, beratung.
awayte, 408, aufwartung.
awhaped, 168, bestürzt, verzagt.

bavme, 27, balsam.
berel, 37, Beryll.
besy, 241, geschäftig, eifrig.
Bole, 3, stier.
bollyn, 101, angeschwollen.
borned, 34, poliert, glänzend.
borowe, 12, bürge.

celured, 52, überwölbt.
clepe, 285, rufen.
costey, 36, entlang geben.
cure, 53, 428, bedecken.

deaurat, 597, golden.
delful, 184, 212, trauervoll, betrübt.
delyuer, 164, frisch, flink.
destreyned, 133, geplagt.
dite 606, 667, gedicht.
dress, 202, sich anschicken.

enclose, 39, einhägen.
endyte, 196. 609, sagen.
espye, 148, erspähen.
eure, 151, 482, geschick.

felle, 97, wild.
fere, 55, Brand.

feruent, 55, heiss.
file, 253, 441, schärfen, schleifen.
firre, 73, kiefer.
forcast, 236, gekürzt.

grene, 33, frisch.
greyn, 90, korn, saat.
grounde, 225, partic. zu grinden, bedrücken, quälen.
gruching, 554, murren.
gruffe, 167, mit dem gesichte vorwärts liegend, platt.

haunce, 430, erhöhen, erheben.
hulfer, 139, stechpalme.
hywe, 31, 132, farbe.

iupartyng, 419, aufs spiel setzen.

lame, 606, schwach.
large, 329, freiheit, belieben.
launde, 120, lustgebüsch.
laurer, 65, lorbeer.
legys, 384, vassallen.
lycour, 29, flüssigkeit.

meynt, 238, 457, vermengt.
motele, 72, farbenpracht.
mys, 603, falsch.

orysont, 6, horizont.
ouer-sprad, 51, bedeckt.

pensifhede, 102, schwermut.
perce, 101, vernichten.
pereles, 346, ohne gleichen.
persaunt, 28, 358, 591, 613, durchdringend.
philbert, 68, haselnuss.
pitte, 92, quelle.
pyne, 64, fichte.

quake, 181, zittern.
quyte, 397, 401, zurückgeben, be-
  lohnen.

refreyn, 341, abstehen.
rent, 220, zerrissen.
respite, 403, in ruhe lassen.
resseyt, 226, behälter.
rowes, 596, strahlen.

sawte, 418, sturm.
sclaundre, 261, verläumden.
sheuer, 46, zerfallen.
shroude, 147, verbergen.
sleghtly, 255, schlau, tückisch.
spere, 56, sphäre, kreislauf.
splay, 33, entfalten.

sute, 82, gruppe.
swogh, 153, ohnmacht.

tapites, 51, teppiche.
tore, 222, zerrissen.

vre, 301, that.
wage, 397, belohnung.
wan, 131, bleich.
welapayed, 549, zufrieden.
wile, 255, list.
wodebynde, 129, geissblatt.
wreche, 471, rache.
wreke (particip), 284, 663, gerächt.
wrest, 48, zwängen.

ynde, 126, blau, indigo.

Namenliste.

Vita.

Ich, Emil, Otto, Johannes Krausser, ev., sohn des †
kaufmanns Emil Krausser und dessen ehefrau Sophie geb.
Farnbacher, wurde am 4. Juli 1872 zu Pforzheim geboren.
Meinen ersten unterricht erhielt ich in der bürgerschule zu
Schwäb.-Gmünd. Vom jahre 1881 an besuchte ich das real-
gymnasium in Mannheim, das ich im jahre 1891 mit dem
zeugnis der reife verliess. Einem lange gehegten wunsche
folgend begab ich mich im herbst 1891 nach Heidelberg, um
mich dem studium der neueren sprachen zu widmen. Hier
hörte ich die vorlesungen der herren professoren und docenten
Braune, Bülbring, Erdmannsdörffer, Kuno Fischer,
Ihne, Kahle, Fr. Neumann, Osthoff, Schick, Schnee-
gans, Uhlig und Wunderlich und nahm an den seminar-
übungen der herren professoren Braune, Bülbring, Ihne,
Neumann und Schick teil.

Während der sommerferien 1894 hielt ich mich in England auf, um die zur vorliegenden ausgabe nötigen hs. und
drucke des Britischen museums, der Bodleiana zu Oxford und
der Pepys-Library zu Cambridge zu copieren. Für die gütige
überlassung der mss. mögen die verwaltungen dieser bibliotheken
bestens bedankt sein.

Zum schlusse ist es mir eine angenehme pflicht, meinen
hochverehrten lehrern, insbesondere herrn prof. dr. Schick,
der mir während der abfassung meiner arbeit in liebens-
würdigster weise rat erteilte, für ihren anregenden unterricht
meinen herzlichsten dank auszusprechen.

www.ingramcontent.com/pod-product-compliance
Lightning Source LLC
Chambersburg PA
CBHW032356020726
47499CB00008B/2779